OFF Course
Episode 01: It Takes Time
AM De la Rosa

CONTENTS

Proceed With Caution

Off Course includes explicit sexual content. Although the author will always write these scenes with enthusiastic consent in mind, the couples involved also have safe words. This series will reference sex heavily, but if you prefer to skip sex scenes, avoid chapters 10 and 14. For plot-relevant information from these chapters, see "Fast Forward...."

This episode...

Fictional religious imagery

Priest turned whore (and proud)

Age gap relationship

Casual attitudes about death

Casual attitudes about pain

Homicidal regent turned whore (and proud)

Liberal use of cigarettes and alcohol

Alien porn

Human porn

Unethical science

Tech bro turned whore (and he's a little shy, but mostly proud)

Shapeshifting for pleasure

Magic for pleasure

Body horror

Unhealthy coping mechanisms

Bodyguard turned whore (and proud)

Bad words

Ass eating

Medical content

This series...*

Mentions of child neglect and abuse

Depictions of medical trauma

Depictions of parental loss

Depictions of homicide

Depictions of abuse of power

The warning list may expand along with the series.

GLOSSARY

- **Alqen** /al-ken/ - a planet in the Kratos galaxy. Its surface is made of aetherite, a mineral that looks like crystal. Its atmosphere is very cold. Qintaril originate from Alqen.

- **Chorister** - a follower of the Radiant Choir.

- **Comm** - short for *communicator*. A portable device similar to a cell phone or smartwatch. Features hologram-projection technology.

- **Conductor** - a champion of the gods for the Radiant Choir. There are eight conductors, each specializing in a different type of magic, respective to the god they champion.

- **Corvora** /core-vore-ah/ - a planet bordering the Milky Way and Kratos Galaxies. Corvora is split into quarterspheres. Corvora Mercy Hospital is on Corvora.

- **Florafolio** - a handheld device for storing and preserving small samples of plant matter.

- **Kratos** - a galaxy neighboring the Milky Way Galaxy. Home to planets such as Corvora and Alqen.

- **Leviathan's Luck** - the official name of the crew's ship and home. Can also refer to the crew together.

- **Nexsus** - large commerce stations. They act as pit stops between planets where spacers can find food, fuel, and lodging.

- **The Prometheus** - also known as "Pim". The crew's submarine-like shuttle takes them on most missions from the ship.

- **Qintaril** /kin-tah-rill/ - or "qin". The native sentient species of Alqen.

- **Radiant Choir** - an Earth religion based around magic. The Radiant Choir believes magic is a gift from the gods. Each of their eight gods represents a different type of magic and the eight notes separating an octave.

- **Sentient** - a general term for humans and aliens.

- **Shuttle** - a flying vehicle suitable for travel on and off-planet.

- **Space Age** - a period in Earth history where Earth explored space.

- **Sterillis Planets** - often followed by a Roman numeral, these planets are found within the Milky Way Galaxy and deemed to be unsuitable for sentient life.

- **Tsytaas** - /sigh-tas/ planet in the undercurrent of the Riptide Galaxy. Part of Tsytaas exists underwater. Tsytaans originate from Tsytaas.

- **Tsytaans** - /sigh-tans/ The native sentient species of Tsytaas. These semi-aquatic aliens can breathe on land and underwater.

- **Terran** - a general term for residents of Earth.

Please note: The character Havoc uses he/him and they/them pronouns interchangeably.

Dedications

To my spouse. Without you, I am lost in space. You are my guiding star.
And to you. Thank you for giving this book a chance. Enjoy your trip!

*"Aging is an extraordinary process where-
by you become the person that you always
should have been."*

David Bowie

A Funeral: On Ice
Chapter 01

//Vince

No cold was more bitter than space. Not winters in New York or trips to Los Lamentos. Not even a walk through the Veil itself was colder.

How the architect of Leviathan's Luck managed a survivable temperature onboard the spaceliner deserved some sort of award. It couldn't have been easy with all that metal. When Vince Luque first saw the spacecraft, he mistook it for a cruise ship parked atop a warehouse in Brooklyn. Vince fought his ingratitude and the desperate desire to beg the captain to turn up the thermostat.

He woke up shivering every morning of his first week on board. A silk robe and matching pants in a dark and psychedelic pattern weren't doing much to keep him warm, but at least he looked hot.

Regardless of the temperature, sleeping in always proved challenging for Vince after thirty-five years of early mornings. This morning he sat alone, trying to squash any fears about being frozen in a block of ice. Considering the other horrific possibilities waiting just outside the spacecraft's doors, he figured frostbite was a relatively merciful end. He tried to keep this in mind as he sat in the conversation pit, chin in palm, staring through an imposing wall of glass. In the dark, the crimson cushions appeared almost chocolate. *Don't think about food.*

His new bedroom was a split level, and the windowed wall lining the steps to the bed area looked out into the vast nothingness of the Milky Way Galaxy. Anyone not trapped inside a floating coffin might marvel at the hazy gleam of far-off stars, clouds of glimmering dust, wonderful cerulean, fuchsia, and citrine between rifts of total darkness. Perhaps Vince could better appreciate its beauty through a telescope and from the safety of the Earth.

How could anyone sleep with this terrifying visual beside them? Lochlan knew the secret. Vince could hear him now, sleeping like a log on the upper-level, though he sounded more like a wood chipper. Without the nasal strip, people probably could have heard Lochlan's snoring galaxies over. It was cute, in a weird way.

Vince kept his laughter low, but his stomach rumbled loudly again. He mock-punched his own torso. Sadly, magic couldn't change the fact that he still needed to eat.

He turned away from the window to the door. The exit stared back at him with hostility. It would be a quick trip. He just needed, like, a granola bar and some water or something. No big deal.

Then again....

Vince ascended the steps to their bed to admire a more serene vision–Lochlan tucked beneath maroon covers.

The older man had a certain timeless ruggedness about him. He was a mountain of a man; fair-skinned, with a snowy peak of lush white hair, and a jawline like a cliff's edge. Thick brows added intensity to his forest gaze.

Lochlan's arms lay across the comforter. Scars decorated his body, aside from his metal arm and leg, where there were small nicks and dents. Tenderly, Vince traced the signs of a life spent in action.

He loved how comfortable Lochlan looked. It had only been a week since their wedding and Vince's subsequent move in, but Lochlan settled in to having Vince around like he'd always been there. It made leaving Earth all the easier.

Vince gently shook Lochlan. It was way too early for him to be awake, and Vince didn't *want* to disturb his husband, but he was not going out there alone.

Heavy-lidded, Lochlan turned to face Vince. With a voice still groggy from sleep but besotted with affection, he grumbled out a "Morning, sweetheart," before planting his stubble on Vince's bare side.

"Good morning, *mi cielo*." Vince's soft accent echoed his upbringing in Mexico. He rubbed his husband's back. "I'm sorry. Did I wake you?"

"Yeah, shaking a guy around will do that to him." Lochlan tried to fight his heavy eyelids, but lost.

"Oh no! I had no idea! Hey, do you want something to eat?"

Lochlan huffed out a drowsy chuckle. "No, but I take it you do."

Vince squirmed. "I promise I will get over this. Eventually."

"Alright. I'm up," Lochlan yawned into a slump. Rubbing the sleep from his eyes, he said, "You know they're not gonna bite you, right? Well, Maynard won't."

"I know. I just want to give them a little time first...to get used to it."

"Don't take it personally. Their issue is with me."

"Ha. Their 'issue' is that you *married* me."

Lochlan took Vince's smaller hand to help him out of bed. "They think I'm irresponsible."

"They think *I'm* a *gold digger*. And the worst part is that I don't blame them! If my friend got married to someone after three months of knowing them, I'd freak out too. Especially considering...." Vince pointed back and forth between himself and Lochlan to hint at the obvious.

Lochlan dropped Vince's hand and held his own out like a shield. "Don't say it." He hated acknowledging their age difference. "I promise they're nice guys once you get to know them. They're just not so great with people. New people especially."

Now, *that* was obvious. Vince recalled their very first meeting; Maynard, Havoc, and about a thousand majorly invasive questions. At one point, Maynard asked Vince for his blood type and measurements. What was he planning to do with that information? To be fair, Vince's first meeting with Lochlan wasn't anymore charming, the cranky geezer.

Vince chuckled. "So you got all the charisma then? Gods help you all."

Lochlan held up his hands to confess. "Hey, last I checked, I hit sixty and still got the sexiest thing in the universe crawling into my bed," he said, dreamy gravel in full effect.

Vince felt a stirring in his lap as he was tugged into a simmering kiss. It didn't matter how many times they had kissed before; when that rough scar on Lochlan's lip brushed against Vince's soft mouth, it always gave him butterflies.

"Well, if it's your bed, then that was already happening long before I got here, Mr. Murdock." Vince gently nipped at Lochlan's bottom lip, earning himself a shudder of delight. It would be worth enduring all the awkwardness in the universe if every morning was going to be like this. Only Vince's rumbling stomach prevented him from pushing Lochlan over for a repeat of last night's activities. "Okay, let's go. Before I chew your arm off."

Lochlan laughed at the way Vince dashed down the steps toward their closet. It was on the lower level, supporting their bed. The massive walk-in was among the few things Vince appreciated about his new accommodations. He couldn't believe this room was nearly empty when he moved in, save for some quality pieces that he praised Lochlan over. Lochlan just stared at Vince like he was speaking another language. A vintage Carhartt hung on a hook unceremoniously. Lochlan had no clue what a gaggle of gays in the Lower East Side would do to get their hands on a jacket like that.

Vince, on the other hand, worshiped his painstakingly collected vintage clothing like he'd built an altar in their closet. Lochlan liked to poke fun. "You time travel from fifty years ago?" he'd ask. To be fair to Vince, the second-hand magazines and CDs he smuggled into the monastery as a boy weren't the latest, but he loved them. Some might turn to books or movies for escapism. Vince had clothes. With the careful consideration of a man choosing his burial suit, he started pulling things from the drawers.

"Nobody cares what you're wearing," Lochlan said. He leaned against the closet doorway, having rolled out of bed in gray striped boxers and a white tank top. The only adornment to the outfit was a red plaid robe with gray trim. At least his slippers matched. Having lived with his best friends as a bachelor for so long, the crew was undoubtedly used to seeing each other at their homiest. Vince's pride demanded better.

"Wrong. *I* care what I'm wearing. If I catch my reflection in something and I don't like it, we're all going to have a bad day. I'm doing this for the sake of the galaxy!"

Lochlan joined Vince in admiring the mirror's reflection. "Galaxy's safe. You're always gorgeous."

Vince leaned into his husband's warm, towering body. "Thank you. And you're welcome!"

"They're gonna love you."

"Well, yeah. I mean, just look at that face." Vince smiled at himself in the mirror. He brought his lips to the back of the pendant around his neck, breathing in the sweet and woody resin within as he murmured a small prayer for courage. "Okay, let's do this."

Lochlan held out his arm. "After you."

Vince made for the door, his confident stride halted by a shrill voice and the sound of high heels clicking in the hall. *Fuck. Havoc.* While Vince could tolerate Maynard's grumpy demeanor, Havoc was a different story. One classified for the horror section.

"Actually." Vince spun around. He walked his fingers up Lochlan's chest. "Maybe...I'm hungry for something else." He pushed Lochlan's chest, and the larger man graciously pretended that actually did something, backing toward the conversation pit.

"Well, you look good enough to eat." Lochlan slung his arms around Vince's waist and pulled him over the back of the couch into a delicious kiss, which succeeded in immediately distracting both of them.

Vince could even ignore the strange noises from the hall thanks to it. It took a few moments for him to realize someone was knocking.

Lochlan removed his mouth from Vince only long enough to shout, "Come back later." Vince giggled into their next kiss.

"Lochlan, meeting." Maynard's assertive voice sounded from the other side of the door.

"Later!" Lochlan repeated, then buried his face in Vince's neck.

"There is a distress signal *now*. Come on."

Lochlan looked out with sudden urgency. Without a word, he tumbled off the couch and marched toward the sliding door. "A distress signal?" he asked. Vince saw Maynard and ducked behind the couch.

Maynard cleared his throat. "Yeah...it's—uh, it's flickering."

Half-nude and crouched behind the couch, Vince felt like a younger version of himself. It reminded him of all the evenings he spent sneaking off the cathedral grounds to plunge into Mexico City's buzzing nightlife. He would have killed for one of those prayer pillows right about now. How much longer could he hold this pose? He was fit but no longer a younger man, he and his knees saddled with the responsibility of leading the entire congregation in morning prayers. Right now, he was a man very much in his thirties—and feeling it—trying not to get caught with his pants down.

Maybe he should just stand. It was spring, after all. Bruises were not an ideal accessory to a pair of shorts.

Maynard and Lochlan's whispers carried across the room. Vince couldn't help but wonder if it might be about him. Perhaps another lecture on shared spaces, or a reminder to keep it down. Lochlan tapped his wrist comm to Maynard's. A small ping signaled an information transfer.

"I'll set up the nav," Lochlan said, reviewing whatever had popped up on screen.

"Thank you. I'm going to let Havoc know," Maynard said. "Please, um—never mind." And with that, the captain was off.

Lochlan turned back toward the room. "You can come out now."

"Thank the Gods," Vince stood, dusted his knees, and checked them for bruises. "Did Maynard, um...?"

"Yeah, I think maybe he noticed." Lochlan pointed at the top of his head, his hair tousled by the fistful and a red glowing bite on his lip. Vince realized Lochlan had also answered the door with no shirt on and his fly down.

Smooth, Vihito. Vince brought his palms to his forehead. "*Why* did you answer the door like that?"

"I don't have anything he hasn't seen before." Lochlan waved, heading for their closet.

A few dull cracks in his spine and a deep groan sounded when he stretched. Since he moved in, Vince noticed how stiff his husband's metal limbs were in the morning but didn't ask. He worried it might be rude. Even if they were married, the relationship was fresh. Vince was still finding a balance; he understood he had a tendency to 'fuss' and that Lochlan was more than capable enough to handle himself. Still, it wasn't easy to see his husband in any amount of pain. Especially not easy when the wild magic condition he'd been born with made his emotions so apparent. Against his will, an aurora conjured around Vince. He swatted it away.

Lochlan stepped back out into the room in jeans and a knit t-shirt. Henley, jacket, and boots in hand, he sat down to put his socks on. He seemed excited. The fine lines that gave his face a distinguished look deepened gorgeously when he smiled. Vince, powerless to stop himself, went in for another kiss, and Lochlan readily accepted it.

With a jerked motion, Lochlan brought his hands to Vince's shoulder before pushing himself away. "Fuck," he panted. "I can't."

Vince, still reeling from the whiplash of excitement, looked Lochlan up and down. "Wait, you're dressed."

"Yeah."

"Why are you dressed?"

Lochlan's face wrung with guilt, a smile still positioned to soften the blow. "We got a job."

"A job? Like, just now?" Lochlan nodded. Vince had been told—repeatedly—about the crew's fast pace. When it was on, it was on, and he would need to brace himself for things to change at a moment's notice. Still, no harm in asking. "And you have to start right this second?" Vince flashed a flirtatious grin and leaned forward, allowing his shirt to drape further off his torso.

Lochlan's chest stilled and his eyes screwed shut to block off the enticing visual. "Believe me, this is torture," he groaned. "But someone might actually be in trouble."

Vince retreated with a sympathetic smile. "Okay. I get it." He really did. He'd spent most of his life in dedication to serving others, which made him no stranger to emergency calls.

Like when the summons bell chimed at three o'clock on a humid September morning years ago, forcing Vince from his rectory behind the cathedral with his cassock thrown on over his pajamas.

The call came from a stumbling birthday party requesting sacrament. They cried out to him, fearing for their sick friend, who might require anointing, or worse, last rites. He sang her a hymn, laid an oiled hand on her forehead to assess her life energy, and chuckled. She wasn't dying; she just had too much to drink. After she threw up in the aisle, they used the crackers to soak up the liquor in her stomach.

Others may have found it annoying, but their joyful expressions upon realizing she was safe and their laughter at the absurdity of it all made it a rewarding evening. Overwhelmed with blessings, the party sang, and Vince happily joined. Any good Chorister should.

Sometimes, when Vince found himself alone with his thoughts, he secretly wished he could find that sense of purpose again. But he was retired now—and for good reason. He had plenty of time to find a new place in life. In the meantime, how could he deny Lochlan that kind of fulfillment?

Vince re-buttoned his knit top. "So I'll just hang out here then?"

Lochlan's smile looked relieved. "Yeah! You've got free rein of the place, but if you're going into the shop, don't touch anything, alright?" Vince couldn't tell if the workshop was more physically dangerous or if Lochlan feared Maynard's reaction to his things being rifled through.

Vince rarely left his new room to avoid Lochlan's roommates. *Our roommates*, he reminded himself. It never occurred to him that he could go anywhere. There had to be an unspoken rule about restricted areas, 'for authorized personnel only.'

This could give him a much-needed opportunity for privacy and a chance to explore the diverse rooms on the spaceliner. Leviathan's Luck held a living room, gym, and library. You'd have to be as dead as a coffin nail not to be a little curious about the trophy room. Something on this giant vessel could keep his body preoccupied. Until Lochlan could come home and find something for it to do. Actually, the prospect of snooping was exciting.

"How long will you be gone?"

Lochlan scratched his chin. "Could be a few hours? Maybe a day?"

"A *day*?!" Vince felt the bubbling arousal inside him dying down.

"...Or two," Lochlan mumbled. Shock forced out a scoff. Seeing Vince's deflated expression, Lochlan quickly made his way back to the couch. "I know. That's just kind of how it is. I won't really have a good idea until we get there." He took his husband's face in his hands. "I'll do my best to keep you in the loop, Vino. Promise."

"I really do understand." Vince ran his fingertips up Lochlan's forearms, sending small shivers up the natural limb. "I'll just stay here...missing you...." He took Lochlan's hand and brought his lips to the palm. "...Looking forward to picking up where we left off."

Every follicle on the arm stiffened. "This better be important, or *I'm* sending out an SOS," Lochlan said. A soft moan slipped past Vince's lips as Lochlan forced them apart in one final, searing kiss. His tongue pushed through, hot and rushed, as if he were trying to burn the shape of Vince's mouth to his memory. "I gotta go set up the navigation, okay?"

He vanished before the warmth did. Vince's teasing *so* backfired. It was just cruel to leave him in such a state. He would pay Lochlan back for that later.

Vince lay on the couch, fiddled with his pendant, and asked himself whether he should find it more impressive or disturbing how quickly Lochlan could compartmentalize. It was horrifying to consider that these types of interruptions might become a regular occurrence.

Vince whispered to himself a reminder to stay spirited, "*Me aviento.*" The distance between the Earth and here was about as big a leap as he could ever imagine.

Old Men Texting
Chapter 02

//Lochlan

Against a backdrop of endless night, the stars winked at Lochlan Murdock, their warm welcome home to the pilot. The helm was his place to shine, and the cosmic view from the windows lining the short hallway never got old. He hadn't seen this room in a week, too busy enjoying his 'honeymoon.' While he'd love to be with his new husband right now, part of Lochlan was excited to get back to work. Travel had been the truest love of his life before Vince arrived.

He approached the central console and took his seat at the instrument panel, rubbing his palms together. Displays, switches, and buttons lit up the dashboard like a pinball machine. He tapped his comm to the reader, sending the coordinates Maynard had given him to the primary display.

"Huh." Lochlan gnawed his inner cheek and double-checked the details.

The crew would find themselves in orbit of Sterillis III. One of the few things Lochlan remembered learning in school was that scientists named the Sterillis line of planets for their emptiness. No one could survive the extreme conditions on these planets. Some spacers even warned against entering the exosphere.

Lochlan scratched his head. No surprise that if someone found themselves out there, they'd find themselves in danger too. What impressed him was that anyone would have the guts to fly out there in the first place. He sent a copy of the route to Maynard and waited for a reply.

PIERCE

Lochlan,
I have reviewed the route. Proceed.
Thank you, Dr. Maynard Ambrose Percival
Sent from my comm, 03/28 9:38AM

Not reading all that

Lochlan, having honed in on 'proceed' and nothing else, spoke into his comm. "Prepare for takeoff." His voice boomed over the speakers throughout the ship. By muscle memory, he pressed the buttons and pulled the levers necessary to bring the engines to life. The hull's soft vibrations signaled to the crew that they would soon set sail. "All systems green." Lochlan reeled in the anchor, the grappling hook keeping them attached to a public docking lot. Everything was set. "Good morning, crew. This is your pilot speaking. Vinni, on behalf of me and these other assholes, welcome aboard Leviathan's Luck service to Sterillis III. It's another lovely day here in the Milky Way Galaxy at a cool -270°C. We're expecting a clear flight to the middle of nowhere. If you look to your right, you'll see nothing, and if you look to your left, you'll see more nothing. If you need anything from me, hesitate to ask. Thank you, gentlemen, for choosing to fly with us today. We are clear for takeoff. Please sit back, relax, and enjoy your flight." With a loose, one-handed grip of the steering yoke, Lochlan activated the thrusters to propel the ship forward.

He grinned at the incoming text from Vince.

✦✧✦

Lochlan followed the navigation outside the exosphere of Sterillis III. He leaned back, taking in the sight of passing stars and the occasional scene from the TV. Maybe he could have used a little more sleep. This smooth ride was making him—

"What the hell?" Avoiding a sudden stop, Lochlan steered the ship away from the planet's gravitational pull.

The route here had been clear, just as he had called, but when they arrived, he found one side of the planet littered with junk—ice, dust, and rocks. The closer he steered to the distress beacon, the worse it got. He skimmed the ship along the outside edge of the asteroid field in search of the distress beacon's source. Deep in the rubble was a station with its cockpit blown wide open, parts of the vessel floating in a trail of its orbital path. He could make it out, but no way he could bring the ship any closer. Not unless he wanted the crew to become the latest addition to the scrap ring. Lochlan deployed the anchor, tethering the ship to a large asteroid nearby, and messaged Maynard.

Nothing. Lochlan waited a few moments more before losing his patience. He marched back toward the elevator, wagering that Maynard was in the lab. If not, he had probably passed out somewhere.

While moving through the living floor, Lochlan spotted Vince preparing a meal in the kitchen. *God.* Lochlan was not a religious man, but he would consider Vince a 'glorious creation.' He made even the simple act of pouring milk into a bowl look like a scene right out of a mural.

Long, raven waves artfully framed high cheekbones, pointed ears, and a slender jawline. Smooth tan skin gave his face a statuesque quality. One of Lochlan's favorite things about Vince was his ink-black eyes, so dark they reflected light like mirrors. Charcoal-smudged eyeliner and a small beauty mark framed them. Lochlan brought his eyes down to marvel at Vince's precisely sculpted figure and the seventies-style clothing he loved to collect. A knit sweater and green flared pants hugged in all the right places.

He really looked right out of a time machine in their kitchen. It hadn't changed much since Lochlan moved in decades ago. Vince raved about the room the first time he saw it. "Look at these rounded edges! The mint? The citrus orange? Are you joking? This is my dream," he cried, kissing the island. Vince liked to cook, but this might be his first time in the kitchen since moving in, and now he looked like he wanted out.

"Fuck!" Vince's sudden shout tore Lochlan from his visit to the museum. He stumbled back. A snake with red, yellow, and black bands slithered onto the counter. He threw the cereal box at it, sending flakes flying. In retaliation, the snake bore sharp fangs and hissed at him.

Lochlan didn't hesitate, rushed in, slammed a hand on the snake's back, and threw it against the cabinets. "Havoc!"

A flash of energy, like lightning trapped in glass, transformed the snake into a humanoid. Havoc's sinister grin turned up from wild green hair. Lochlan reached into the nest.

"Crap," Havoc winced as they were slammed into the pantry door.

The way Vince threw himself over Lochlan's arm in defense of Havoc had Lochlan feeling like he'd committed a crime. "Oh, he's *fine*." Lochlan dropped them.

Landing hard on his ass, Havoc doubled over in pain. "That really hurt!" With a sharp nail pointed at Lochlan, Havoc cried to Vince, "This is the type of violent brute you married, Father!"

Lochlan rolled his eyes. Havoc should count themself lucky. If Vince weren't here, they'd already be in the garbage disposal.

Crouching down, Vince naively checked for injuries. "I'm *so* sorry. Are you okay?"

"Oh, I think I'm alright. I just—" Havoc cried in agony, using their shapeshifting ability to bend their spine completely in half.

Vince stumbled back onto his hands. "Oh my Gods!"

Lochlan wondered how well magic could fix something like that in an actual emergency. Luckily, they wouldn't have to find out. He grabbed Havoc's collar, lifted them into the air, and shook them like a rag. "Knock it off!"

Havoc released the form, howling with laughter as they fixed their spine. "Okay, okay! Relax. I'm fine, Father, see?"

Vince was pale as a ghost. "I—I think I'm gonna go lay down." With weak knees, he used the counter to support himself and stumbled out of the kitchen.

Lochlan normally enjoyed pranks, but this one went too far. The moment he knew Vince was going to make it on his own, he shoved Havoc. "What the hell is the matter with you?"

Havoc grinned, rubbing the sore spot on their shoulder. "I'm training our new puppy. Like you asked!"

"That's not what I said!" Out of the corner of Lochlan's eye, he spotted Maynard enter and swiftly turn back around. "Hey, come control your idiot!"

Maynard flinched. After forty-five years of friendship, Lochlan didn't need to see Maynard's face to know that he was considering running away. Maynard turned toward the crew with a sigh. "You're making a lot of racket...."

"Did you fall asleep? I texted you."

Maynard pushed his glasses. "No...."

Lochlan searched Havoc's face for the truth. Havoc nodded. Of course. Maynard wasn't a night owl or a morning bird. He was more like a seabird, flying for so long without rest that when he finally lost to sleep, he could be out for a whole day.

He straightened into a captain's stance. "Havoc, what happened with Vincent was uncalled for. Clean this mess up and apologize." Maynard's attempt to deflect didn't fool Lochlan, but he appreciated the backup.

Havoc tossed their head back, unconcerned. "You wanted us to be 'friends,' right? What's more friendly than a harmless prank?"

Lochlan opened the pantry and grabbed the first ready-to-eat things he spotted: a wadded-up bag of salt and vinegar chips, animal crackers, and a strawberry protein bar. Not a 'balanced' meal but it would have to do. "Me and Pierce are used to your bullshit by now."

"Ha! Don't act so cool. You still fall for it all the time." Havoc pinched Maynard's cheek. "Isn't that right, starlight?"

"Darling." Maynard stuffed down a blush. "Shapeshifting is a one-in-a-trillion type of ability. Vincent has never seen someone do what you can. It's jarring." Havoc pouted at his boyfriend, batting his eyelashes. Lucky prick caught Maynard on a morning where he was too tired to fight back. "And Lochlan...you know how Havoc is." He waved, as if that was all the explanation needed.

"Nice, Pierce. Way to exercise that authority." Lochlan bumped into Maynard's shoulder on his way back to his room. "I sent you the course. I'll be right back. And you—" With a look wedged between begging and threatening, he pointed at Havoc. "Play nice. Come on, for me?"

"The *nicest*," Havoc sang. Lochlan didn't buy that, but he had to check on his walking target of a husband before the crew took off.

He cursed under his breath the whole way down the hall. Like it wasn't bad enough that his friends were giving him a hard time, now they were picking on Vince too. *Definitely should have seen that coming.* He tapped the touchpad by the door with his elbow.

He paused, closed it, and opened it again.

The door revealed what was supposed to be his room, but it looked more like one in a haunted house; much colder and darker than he left it. Light bulbs flickered with surges of energy. Twisted beams of eerie green magic shrouded every family photo, model car, and magazine. Ghoulish wisps with long, sorrowful faces like skulls circled Vince, who was levitating still as a statue beneath a ghostly veil.

"Fucking hell," Lochlan boomed.

The statue turned to face him, back tattoo glowing the same spectral white as his eyes. "Oh, hey!" The magic disappeared, and the room returned to normal as Vince cheerily lowered to the ground.

"Am I...interrupting something?" Lochlan wasn't sure he wanted the answer.

Vince tilted his head. "I was meditating. The Veil is very calming." It was like he was talking about taking a stroll through the park.

"How the hell does that make anyone feel calm? I thought I walked into Halloween Horror Nights."

"Ha ha," Vince said flatly. His annoyed expression faded when he pointed to the pile of food Lochlan was holding. "Please say that is for me."

Lochlan held out the stash. "Yes, *Carrie*, it's for you." On a regular morning, he would have loved to spoil Vince, take him out for breakfast, or make something at home. Still, these random snacks earned a halo of stars conjured by Vince's magic reacting with his joy.

"You're so good to me." Vince scratched beneath Lochlan's chin. Lochlan melted into the affectionate palm. *Pretty... shiny*. His comm buzzed.

"Can't stay long, Vino." Lochlan cleared some space on the bar to set the snacks down. "Real quick, about this morning...."

Vince grunted, the crown of stars disappearing. "You mean the super funny way Havoc tried to kill me?"

"That's how they make friends." It wasn't a joke. Lochlan thought back to their first meeting. The mission was to thwart Havoc's evil—well, maybe not evil so much as irritating—schemes. Their confrontation came to blows and after being peeled from the rubber of Lochlan's boot, Havoc, the sleazy siren, escaped the mission with a new place to live, a new friend, and a new love interest. Although, Lochlan was having serious second thoughts about being a friend this morning. "When we first met, Havoc *actually* tried to kill me and now look at us!"

Vince's eyes narrowed. "Is that...supposed to make me feel better?"

"Oh, don't worry, I'm fine."

With the way Vince's neck craned back, he looked like he was sighing at his gods. "I guess I just have to get over it. I'm so used to trusting my own eyes, odd as that might seem."

The red flags were rising. Lochlan knew what it was like when Vince hit his boiling point and it would not be fun. The crew's resident bodyguard could guarantee no one's safety if that happened.

Lochlan took both of Vince's hands. "Try not to take anything they do too seriously. Or you'll be turning our room into a twenty-four-hour theme park," he joked, trying to force a smile out of his husband. The faintest curl tugged the corner of Vince's lip, so Lochlan went on, "Fine. Have it your way. Guess I'll quit mercenary work and run the park full time. We'll make a fortune. Gotta upcharge because you're so damn handsome."

With Vince, flattery could get you anywhere. He lowered his eyelids, smirking coyly. "*Our* room. So cute," he gushed. Lochlan's comm buzzed again. Did Maynard really need to write out a single question mark like a goddamn letter? "Go on," Vince said, planting a kiss on Lochlan's cheek. "I'm fine.

❖✧❖

To account for the colossal hole in the station's hull, the crew would need oxygen suits. They assembled in the Keel, the garage-style entrance and exit to the ship, which housed their lockers and vehicles. Lochlan stood in front of his locker, fastening a white-banded belt around his jumpsuit. He glanced at his reflection, inspecting the closures around his metal limbs.

This suit had served him well over the years. Sure, it was durable. More importantly, who could resist a man in uniform? The steel buckle showcased a sea serpent's head, a detail Lochlan personally requested. Separating the top and bottom created the illusion of light earthy brown pants with a sand and stone block toned jacket. Quilted panels, piping, and steel shielded their weak points, and the ship's signature orange accents filled Lochlan with pride.

He loaded his tactical bag with a change of clothes, individually packaged meals in small foil pouches, and basic toiletries. They fit within the leather cylinder. He adjusted the four straps into pairs so that the pack would sit diagonally across his back. After thirty years of work, he'd learned less was best. As far as the pilot and bodyguard was concerned, all he needed for most missions were his own two hands.

"Okay. I believe we have everything we need." Maynard hoisted a bulky bag of random gadgets over his shoulder. No matter the mission, he was always over-prepared.

"You two take forever." Havoc packed their bag with shower supplies and not much else, the rest of the space saved for 'souvenirs.'

From behind Lochlan, a small voice piped up. "Is there anything I can help with?" It was Vince. Lochlan wouldn't have guessed it with that timid tone.

He reached a hand out, inviting his husband to come closer. "We're alright, Vinni. Thank you."

"Well, this is...serious." Vince poked the corrugated tubing, which ran from Lochlan's helmet, down his chest, and took a sharp turn at his waist to an oxygen tank on his opposite hip. "Is that enough food?" Vince asked, side-eyeing the bag. Must have been a sight to see; Lochlan usually ate like a horse. "I could make you something."

"Havoc doesn't eat on missions. This is sufficient." Maynard hadn't even looked up from his comm to deliver the icy explanation.

Havoc popped up behind Vince, startling him. "That's May's subtle way of telling you to butt out."

"Ignore them." Lochlan positioned himself between his friends and his husband. He tucked a strand of hair behind Vince's ear and tilted his chin up to smolder, "Hey...."

"I'll miss you too," Vince whispered. The honey-sweet kiss he pulled Lochlan into was tough to pull away from. This mission had to be fast. Lochlan needed more of this.

Maynard cleared his throat.

Havoc tugged Lochlan by the arm. "You can play more later, Laney. Wouldn't want to be left behind, would you?"

"Is that an option?"

Vince stayed put, giving a small goodbye wave as the crew climbed into the shuttle. A pang of guilt hit Lochlan as he took one last good look at his husband. Crap. This was their first time apart since the wedding. He probably should have asked Vince how he felt.

From inside the shuttle, Maynard groused, "Maybe this is one of those 'non-urgent' distress beacons?"

Lochlan scowled at the waiting crew. "Alright, let's make this quick."

Outdoor Voices Only

Chapter 03

//Maynard

Maynard Percival could not wait to be free from the shuttle. From the moment the crew left, Havoc and Lochlan fought over the radio. After five minutes of continuous yelling reverberating off the windows, Maynard exercised his captain's privileges to play tie-breaker, forcing cool jazz on his companions. He believed the soft melodies would do well to soothe the bickering children. He was wrong.

"Are we there yet?" Havoc whined as if he weren't old enough to be someone's father.

Lochlan jammed the yoke, yelling, "Think I won't turn this around?!" and sounding very much like an actual father. Not that any of them would understand what that sounded like.

"*Where* is the ibuprofen?" Maynard growled into his bag. Of course, he had forgotten it again. He remembered a pocket version of *The Art of Science*, yet somehow forgot water or any sort of medication. As if he would have time for drawing.

"There it is," Havoc said.

"Where?" Maynard squinted into the side pocket he thought Havoc was pointing at.

"There." Havoc prodded Maynard's forehead with their finger, grinning. "That adorable throbbing vein you get when you're all fired up."

Maynard shielded his forehead. "Don't be cute."

"We both know that's not possible." Havoc ran their finger through their shortened hair, shifted to better fit in the helmet. With a swing of his legs, he 'accidentally' kicked the back of Lochlan's seat.

"You better not be scratching up my upholstery!" Lochlan barked.

Havoc inspected the back of the seat, grimacing as they obsessively rubbed a spot. He shot Maynard a look of distress. Maynard's eyes flew open. Lochlan loved this damn shuttle more than anything, and he would kill Havoc if there were a scratch. Maybe Maynard could fix it before Lochlan noticed. He leaned over the seat with his heart racing—the seat was fine. Havoc responded to Maynard's glare with a snicker.

Maynard enjoyed vehicles, but the pilot's enthusiasm was unparalleled. Maynard often lent an ear to Lochlan's frustrations over his ancient high school car, which, impressively, he still drove. One of Lochlan's most cherished possessions was this shuttle, the crew's Prometheus Mk. IV Strider or, "Pim" as he affectionately called it.

The Prometheus was a brilliant creation—if Maynard said so himself—a never-ending collaboration between Lochlan and him. Even in the most unstable environments, the heavily armored, all-terrain shuttle could withstand everything from cargo transport to combat flight. Although it was purely aesthetic, they equally valued the orange paint on the leather seats.

"It should look like a submarine," Maynard declared in a parts shop back in Brooklyn some years ago. That day, they first considered creating a shuttle from scratch. "It's suitable for exploration." He pointed to a wide plastic bin on the top shelf.

They could have called over an employee, but Lochlan grabbed it with ease. "What's with the ocean theme?"

"What?" Maynard pulled from the bin a handful of hefty bolts. They were not quite right. The heads reflected a certain cold and corporate minimalism that made his neck stiffen. He shrugged. "I like the ocean."

"You're scared of the ocean." Lochlan continued shuffling through the wall of bins, peeking into random ones.

"Well, I have good reason! Can you believe that we know more about space than we do about Earth's ocean?" Maynard surrendered the unsatisfactory bin. "Regardless, I can find something terrifying and beautiful."

"Perv," Lochlan teased. He preempted Maynard's protest by offering him a bin of bolts with a more nautical look about them. They were perfect.

Maynard elbowed Lochlan, an involuntary smile playing on his lips as he commanded him to shut up.

This memory came to mind every time they worked on the Prometheus together. Perhaps because the teasing over Maynard's newly established relationship had started there and never stopped. Lochlan wasn't exactly wrong. Maynard snuck a glance at Havoc. *Terrifying and beautiful.*

With every move, Havoc's captivating amethyst eyes sparkled. Their iridescent skin, stretched over sharp, slender bones, refracted the shuttle's lights like the scales of a fish. Maynard's decades-long love didn't diminish his fascination with the two horns on Havoc's head, which bloomed like coral emerging from a nest of knee-length, seafoam green hair. Even now, as Havoc sat back with their arms folded and legs swaying, their princely background showed in graceful, flamboyant movements.

It was always amusing to see him in the oxygen suit. His daily attire was a stark contrast to the typical rugged style of a communications officer for a crew of spacers; tall heeled boots, loose blouses exploding with lace and ruffles, lavish coats and pants tailored in strange but stylish silhouettes over a slant figure.

Havoc gasped suddenly.

Maynard raised an eyebrow. "What is it?"

"Did we put Vince in his crate?" He asked, with feigned concern. Maynard checked Lochlan's agitated jaw clench, then shot Havoc a warning look. "I don't want him peeing all over the house!"

Maynard could not be caught laughing at that. Not while Lochlan sat closest to the eject button.

From the outside, Havoc was undeniably lovely. It was their inner beauty that required more time to rear its magnificent head. It was doubtful that Vincent could withstand the wait time. Lochlan's flings rarely lasted that long.

Uncomfortable in his seat, Maynard recalled he had privately tasked himself with a separate mission today: talk to Lochlan about the whole...marriage...thing.

Maynard rubbed his eyes beneath his lenses. God, he would never get used to that–his best friend, married, and to someone so inappropriate. Looking back, one should have expected that of Lochlan. The fool.

Their last conversation over the matter nearly came to blows, but as Havoc had so bluntly reminded Maynard this morning, he and Lochlan shared a bank account. "So, when this inevitably goes to shit..." Havoc completed their statement with a thumbs down.

Truly, it wasn't just about the money. That would come and go. Maynard was more concerned than any-thing about his best friend's mental state. Lochlan's life was a series of unrelenting blows, and he always got up again except for his divorce. Maynard was shocked that after so many years of pushing himself in the opposite direction, Lochlan would come back full force.

The spaces between the steel grate over the shuttle's thick glass nose allowed those in the front seat an immersive view of space. While his crewmates bickered, Maynard found calm in staring out the window, considering the ideal moment for 'the talk.' By some merciful fate, the ride was relatively brief, which meant Maynard could focus on something else.

The Prometheus came before the station. Floating in the middle of an asteroid field, the steel interconnected modules of the craft were identical in size and in the formation of a cross. From the outside, Maynard could easily deduce the station as one designated for medical research by its metal banner featuring the universally recognized emblem of a blue cross. Normally, such banners included a vessel's registration number, but this one only displayed 'Corvora Mercy Hospital' in Universal.

Corvora was not a planet the crew was familiar with, but Maynard knew enough to find it strange that their research station would be all the way out here. The planet was several astronomical units away.

Havoc took point on communications. On their comm, they pulled up a random Corvoran television channel. The comical music and sound effects suggested a cartoon. Maynard watched intently. Havoc's ability to learn languages by listening was just as enchanting as the adorable way their ears twitched while concentrating. Havoc reached for the microphone connected to the shuttle's speaker system and made one last attempt to call in, perfectly adapting the clipped staccato of Corvora's native tongue. Radio silence answered the crew.

Maynard contemplated their options. It was only the station, a nexus, and their shuttle in this corner of space. With one of the station's wings damaged and the other three intact, splitting up would make it easy to find who or what they were seeking.

"Alright, pull in," Maynard said. As instructed, Lochlan positioned their shuttle to dock at the station's center. They heard the metallic clasp of the tower at the top of their shuttle latch onto the station. "Turn the magnets on."

"I *know*," Lochlan groaned, still in a bad mood from earlier. To be fair, they all were.

Havoc's usual provocation was not helpful. "Remember the last time? You forgot the magnets, and the shuttle slid right off the side of that building?" Lochlan, though clearly annoyed, obeyed, and as soon as he secured the shuttle, he opened his comm to make a call.

For a few seconds, the only sound was the rustling of fabric. "What the hell am I doing? Oh! Hello?" Vincent chirped from the other end of the line.

Predictably, the Earthling was not adapting well to using a comm. Cell phones were still the most popular form of communication device back on the crew's home planet, especially amongst young people. As a wedding gift, Maynard had given Vincent his first comm. Vincent simply stared at it blankly and asked if 'cuter' wristband options were available.

Maynard learned one vital fact during his brief acquaintance with Vincent. The man was shallow. Vincent obsessed over his own image, frivolously spent Lochlan's money, and was a born magician with no interest in actually using magic. The former Chorister priest, possessor of universe-altering abilities, traded everything for a life of partying and mail delivery in New York City. Upon meeting Lochlan there, he swiftly singled him out. For what? An allowance? A free place to stay? Maynard struggled to decide if he should feel more impressed or appalled. Lochlan was not normally so easy to target.

"Hey Vino, I just wanted to let you know we got here."

"Just now? Well, that took forever."

Havoc and Maynard exchanged critical glances at the overly dramatic statement. It had been only about twenty minutes since they had left.

"I know. I know. I promise, I'm hauling ass." Lochlan chuckled. "Call you back in a bit."

"Okay, love you!"

"Love you, bye."

"You need to train that out of him or he'll develop separation anxiety." Havoc mocked. Maynard stifled a snort.

"Shove it up your ass."

"He understands we could be here for *days*, right?" Maynard asked, trying not to sound condescending.

The look on Lochlan's face suggested he'd failed. "*Yes. I gave him the heads up. He's just messing around.*"

With an eye roll, each member of the crew donned their white, rounded helmets and climbed the stepladder to the tower. The inside light panel changed from orange to blue, indicating that the airlock was secured. Gravity disappeared following a release of air. Together, they floated into open space toward a side door and an aluminum ladder near the dock, granting Maynard and Havoc station entry. Lochlan continued scaling the station from the outside to investigate the blown-in cockpit.

Once inside, Maynard took note that no one came to greet them. A lifetime ago, he spent his biomechanics research days with his former lab group, working at various medical stations just like this one. The Echelon Group Corp—an absurd name, he knew, but what they lacked in intelligence, they compensated for in funding—possessed the most pristine of stations. Every researcher's dream. This station was about as welcoming as a war zone. Stray papers and various supplies littered the all-white ground. The overhead lights flickered above, but fortunately, the gravity generator was intact.

Maynard picked up a digital clipboard. The plastic frame looked...melted? Crushed, perhaps? Whatever happened to it was no simple feat. Havoc began sifting through the clutter for any information they could read while Maynard took his trusty scanner to different corners of the room.

He did not have the heart to tell his companions that, beside Lochlan's cybernetic limbs, the handheld device was one of his proudest inventions. Maynard never wanted to sound so self-congratulatory, but he considered it a perfect design. *Objectively*.

The handle sat snugly, custom-shaped for his fist. The striking sensor pointed out like the muzzle of a gun. With the satisfying press of a button, two additional screens folded out for optimal job flow. He pulled the antenna out, allowing him a connection to the computer on Leviathan's Luck. The sleek orange and beige casing with dark blue accents gave the entire design that signature 'Dr. Percival' flair. It could do anything and everything he needed; identify the chemical components of any object or atmosphere, act as a remote controller for his other tech—it could even turn the coffee maker on and off.

A few minutes of random scanning later, Lochlan reappeared, sliding down the ladder with a sample in hand. "There's a bunch of stone crammed into the corners up there." He held out a dull brown rock the size of his fist.

Maynard took his scanner to the sample, an orange beam cast over the stone like a net with a gratifying electronic warble. Within seconds, he had information on display: iron and silicate minerals. "Ah. So, it was an asteroid that hit them. Why put a station in the middle of an asteroid field like this?"

"Yeah, how the hell didn't they see that coming?" With hands on his hips, Lochlan puffed out his chest. "Bet you're feeling pretty lucky to have me as a pilot right about now." He winked. Maynard shook his head, suppressing a smile so as not to embolden the arrogance.

Lochlan pointed at the ceiling camera in the corner of the center chamber. His titanium hand broke the rock in half. He handed a piece to Maynard, who understood this as a challenge. The baseball fans lined up next to each other to take turns throwing their rocks. Lochlan whooped when Maynard just missed the bracket holding the camera in place and instead hit the camera itself and cracked the lens. Lochlan pushed Maynard back. Exaggerating his swing, he hit the bracket precisely at the joint, which sent the camera crashing down. He performed a small celebration jog around Maynard as if he were running the diamond on a baseball field. It forced a smile from Maynard. Despite his immaturity, Lochlan had an infectious way of forcing fun on others that made it impossible to stay mad at him.

"Go pick that up, idiot," Maynard chuckled.

Lochlan danced on top of the imaginary home plate. "Hey! This idiot just won the World Series, baby!"

"This is not how baseball works."

"What the hells?" Havoc approached them. "Why am I the only one doing actual work?"

"For once," Lochlan and Maynard said together.

Havoc scoffed. "*I* have the passcode for the doors! *Thank you, Havoc!*"

Maynard placed a hand on his partner's back. "Thank you, darling," he said. Havoc cupped their ear as if waiting for more.

"Nice, Hawk." Lochlan popped open the camera to pull out the memory card from within and handed it to Maynard.

"Okay. I'm ready to leave." Havoc turned to the ladder.

Before they could get far, Lochlan grabbed their arm and swung them back around. "We just got here."

Havoc dropped their head sluggishly. "And I have been carrying this team since the moment we left! I'm exhausted!"

They received a puzzled look from Lochlan. "What's so tiring about reading?"

"Well, if you actually knew how to read, you might understand."

"I can read. I choose not to." Lochlan tapped his index finger on his temple. "I gotta conserve my brain space for important stuff."

With a smirk, Havoc cocked their head and said, "Such as...the shape of Vince's ass?"

Lochlan pointed at his nose, signifying their perfect accuracy. Teenagers could not have laughed any more heartily than they did.

Maynard, with a hidden grin on his face, checked the access history of the northern keypad. For days, he hadn't seen his companions so carefree. Their antics were a welcome sign of normalcy returning. To his surprise, he discovered he actually missed their crude jokes.

Maynard raised a hand to interrupt. "Okay, boys. Settle down. According to the keypad's access history, there are six personnel on board."

"Were," Lochlan amended.

"We don't know that yet." Maynard pointed at Havoc. "South." He then pointed to Lochlan. "East." Finally, he pointed to himself. "West." The crew gave him an understanding nod. "This place is small. It shouldn't take long, but don't rush. We will meet back here in half an hour," Maynard directed.

Lochlan groaned into a stretch. "Sounds good."

"Alright then, starlight."

Relieved to have his crew back, Maynard took a deep breath and prepared to set them off when the ringing of Lochlan's comm interrupted him.

Enter Stage Left
Chapter 04

//Havoc

Havoc turned for their wing of the station. Just as the crew was about to split off, Lochlan's comm rang. Again.

Lochlan's shoulders stiffened as he answered, "Vinni?"

"Lochlan?" Vince's voice came in faster than the picture.

"Hey, sugar. Everything okay?"

The tense shoulders of Vince's tiny hologram lowered. "I called to ask you that." The Father's tone had a sharpness about it, and Havoc felt their ears prickle. Could these finally be the long-awaited seeds of relationship drama? Oh, Havoc *had* to stay back and watch this.

In order to block the rest of the crew from his private conversation, Lochlan turned away. He was the exact kind of stupid to do so while remaining connected to the open communications channel. "Yeah... I'm fine?"

"Okay, I don't mean to sound—whatever." Vince paused. "I just thought you'd call more."

Standing back, Havoc studied Lochlan's profile, the way his brow curled and how he chewed the inside of his cheek between words. Vince did not know Lochlan well enough to pick up on his obvious displays of agitation, but Havoc knew them well.

Havoc taunted Maynard with an 'I told you so' expression. Maynard nodded, wary. Even if he agreed, he was a softer soul and he could not openly root for the collapse of his best friend's marriage. Havoc considered it their responsibility to maintain balance, so they cheered on unrestrained.

"Jeez, Vinni, we just talked and I'm working right now," Lochlan said. Vince just scoffed in response. An uncomfortable silence hung between the couple.

Havoc switched their comm channel to the one between him and Maynard only. "What's the window for marriage annulment on Earth again? Shall we start on the paperwork?"

"That's not how it works," Maynard said. "Do you really think...this is it? I'm not saying I'm relieved if it is, but...if it is...." Then he would be relieved.

Havoc smirked. "It's not exactly record time, but, how many people have waited for Lochlan only to never hear from him again? If Vince can't stand an hour, he won't survive a day."

"Hmmm. When I gave Lochlan the mission brief, he *did* leap off of Vincent pretty quickly. Typical Lochlan. That's got to have Vincent feeling at least a little resentful."

Havoc raised a single brow. "'Leap off of'? What does that mean?" Havoc gasped, realization curling their lips into a titillated grin. "Did you walk in on them?"

Maynard's eyes shot away shamefully. On reflex, Havoc tried to cover their mouth, but the helmet blocked them, so they cackled unfiltered.

"I didn't walk in! I knocked and...Lochlan answered the door." How 'typical Lochlan' indeed.

"Ha! Oh, what are you so ashamed of? He doesn't have anything you haven't seen before."

"We're not talking about this." Maynard fumbled for the controls on his comm to switch him and Havoc back to the crew's open channel.

Vince seemed to have lost this round. "I know you're busy...I just got worried. Can you try to call me back in a few hours? Please?" In Havoc's opinion, this shameless display of begging was far more humiliating than anything Maynard had done.

Lochlan nodded. "Yeah, of course, sweetheart. No problem. Go meditate," he said playfully.

Another chilly silence. "Is that supposed to be funny?"

"Yeah...no." Lochlan cleared his throat. "Uh. I love you? And, uh...you look gorgeous today. Have I told you that?"

"You—" Vince interrupted himself, genuine agitation rolling into mock agitation. "Whatever, I love you too. Call me." The hologram disappeared.

Lochlan refused to look his friends in the eyes. He and Maynard were still, as if a cold draft had frozen them in place. "So...anyway,"

"That was weird, right?" Havoc said, a hot knife through the tension.

"Really?"

Havoc brought their hands to their hips. "We've been gone half an hour. It's a bit much, if you ask me."

"Well, it's a good thing no one fucking asked you," Lochlan spat.

"I'm just saying what we're *all* thinking." Havoc directed the statement to their boyfriend. Lochlan glared at him, too.

Maynard's eyes darted back and forth between them like a tennis ball caught in their rally. "Um." He cleared his throat. "Right. Well. I wonder...what time is it?"

"Come on, man," Lochlan said. "Help me out here."

Maynard stood up straight. "Darling, perhaps we should let Lochlan and Vincent work things out privately." Lochlan gave Havoc a smug look.

With an unsurprised yet annoyed sigh, Havoc gave up, throwing their hands up. "Have it your way."

Maynard put a hand on Lochlan's shoulder. "Lochlan, I know you're feeling upset. However, things aren't always as bleak as they appear...like, um, oh! This reminds me of the lab fire I had the other day!" Havoc stared at Maynard. He did not know where this was going, but it could be nowhere good. Thus, Havoc encouraged Maynard to go on. "You and Vincent are like two highly reactive chemicals. Overdo it and...." He imitated an explosion. Lochlan's eyes grew wide. "Oh, but, uh, maybe that could be a good explosion! A teachable explosion. I mean, you could destroy your life—my lab, I should say. Or you could find a very fun way to...to roast a marshmallow! Anyway. You put in place new fire safety protocols, and you learn what not to do. For next time. So that's what I'm saying; your relationship is like a house fire. No! That doesn't sound right. Let me try again. Right. Just like making a chemical compound, relationships are incredibly difficult...." Havoc began tapping their foot. "But not mine!" He spotted Lochlan's frown and added, "Well, I mean, it's not perfect. Nothing is perfect, though! Certainly not Havoc and I!" Maynard folded his arms and looked down. "I'm done talking."

"Forever?" Havoc asked with a sudden urge to poke a hole in Maynard's suit.

"Okay, stop trying to make me feel better." Lochlan tightened his bag straps and set a timer on his comm. "See you in thirty." He marched off toward his assigned wing.

Havoc looked at Maynard, annoyance painted all over his face. "I know. I—it's his business. Let's just get going."

Havoc sauntered around their assigned wing of the station, making the most of a dull investigation. When Maynard had spun the wheel, it landed Havoc in the south wing, which seemed was simply the living quarters.

The chambers Havoc passed were increasingly uninteresting, and each one was completely devoid of life. He tossed any paperwork he found along the way. The station was a wreck anyhow; adding to the mess was like adding a drop to the ocean. Most of the documents they found were boring, useless medical transcripts. Havoc only learned that the center researched rare diseases, memory loss, and neurological perceptions of time. *Blah, blah, blah.*

He passed the kitchen, stowing away a perfectly fine box of ice cream sandwiches into his bag, along with a single photograph hanging from a magnet. It appeared to be of the station's researchers. Rapid-fire, Havoc shifted into all five forms and tucked the photo into their pocket.

It never hurt to save as much information into his memory as possible. Just in case.

Havoc entered the bedchamber. To pass the time, they considered taking a nap and hoisted themselves onto the top bunk. After a grueling thirty seconds, they decided this was far too understimulating.

What was it about missions lately? They were losing their spark. For a quarter of a century, Havoc had treasured every moment spent with Maynard and Lochlan menacing the public, but this week of ongoing arguments stole Havoc's zeal for work today.

This is Vince's fault. In fact, everything was perfect until the incubus had stowed away. Now Lochlan was no fun to be around. If he were ever around.

Havoc, staring down the barrel of an infinite life, worried that fatigue had already set in. A down-to-your-bones type of tired only other people his age understood. With Maynard and Lochlan by his side, Havoc could put aside these kinds of unpalatable uncertainties, but he could not continue to ignore the obvious. They were getting older.

It was sometime in their fifties when Havoc came at Maynard, with tweezers and a frenzied determination to rid their boyfriend of the ash-colored weeds plaguing his scalp. "Leave my grays alone!" Maynard demanded, knocking the tweezers out of Havoc's hand.

"They're unsightly!" Havoc picked up the tweezers and dusted them off.

Maynard unfurled a tightly wound coil on his beard defensively. "I get a lot of compliments about my hair, thank you."

"I agree you are stunning. Top to bottom!" Havoc folded their arms behind their back, wringing one wrist. "But I don't like the gray. Get rid of it."

"Oh." For a change, it seemed Maynard understood what they were hinting at without them having to admit it. "I'll ask Lochlan to help me dye them."

"You're sure?" Havoc asked, pulled into Maynard's arms.

"Yes."

Havoc wrapped their arms around Maynard's waist and playfully swayed them from side to side. "Green? We'll match!"

"Don't make me change my mind."

Maynard, dutiful boyfriend that he was, dyed his hair consistently for the next five years. It wasn't until the crew stayed off the ship on a longer mission that he missed a month of dyeing and Havoc realized how quickly the grays had taken over. Havoc ordered Maynard to stop dyeing his hair immediately. Maybe it would not have been so shocking if they had seen it coming. They were right so far. By now, they were used to it and, Gods, did Maynard age like a fine wine.

Havoc sighed. One day Maynard and Lochlan wouldn't be here, and then what was Havoc supposed to do? Who would help him pass the time? He had to admit he was an acquired taste. Maybe this was his golden age, and it was all downhill from here. It could be eons of...what? Napping?

Havoc felt an unpleasant sensation in their chest and stomach. They really should go back to Maynard. They'd rather do anything than sit here brooding.

Havoc rolled off the bunk, allowing themself to hit the floor flat on their back. They stayed there for a moment, pain barely registering, when they spotted a journal with a lock underneath the bottom bunk bed.

"Well, hello. What do we have here?" They turned over onto their stomach to swipe the book from its hiding place.

It should belong to a researcher, but it could contain with anything; salacious gossip or the gory details of stomach-churning procedures. Havoc's spirits sank at the idea of it being merely a supply logbook. Regardless, it piqued their interest.

A second search under the bed failed to reveal the key. Kicking their feet in the air, they examined the journal, cheaply made and paper bound. The shoddy lock gave them an idea.

Taking advantage of his shapeshifting ability, Havoc extended one fingernail to a long thin point and fortified the keratin to use it as a lock-pick. After a few seconds of finagling, something clicked inside the keyhole and the lock popped open.

"*Excellent job, Havoc!*" they cheered, to no one. "*Why, thank you, Havoc!*" They began flipping through the lined pages. He'd landed in clover, delighted to find the book was a sort of diary. "Ohh, your captain is going to have a very nice reward for you in his pants when he sees how you—"

Now what in the fresh hell is that?

Sloppily written Corvoran letters spelled out 'CALLED FOR HELP.' The red text filled the page, disobeying margins as if written in a rush. After that, nothing legible. Havoc flipped through the older entries. Initial passages were unassuming, but at a break-neck pace, they became increasingly incoherent. Stars and spirals dotted the edges. An alarming number of the last pages were nothing but the same design of a large spiral in different colors over and over.

Something gave Havoc an unsettled feeling in their stomach again. Although it was entirely possible that this came from eating the six-month-old snacks they'd scavenged.

"Hmmm..." Havoc crinkled their nose at the diary. "Looks good!" They slammed the book shut. Putting their discoveries in their bag, they set off for Maynard.

Right away, they could tell Maynard's wing was likely one dedicated to the actual 'medical research' part of the medical research station. Five desks lined the walls of the first chamber, displaying diagrams and charts written in a language Havoc could read, but with technical jargon they could not.

They scanned the room for Maynard and found him crouching by a desk, scanning the floor.

Maynard was the very picture of brilliance and dignity. Dense hair, more pepper than salt, featured a tiny, charming ocean wave carved into one side. A full beard trailed along his powerful jaw to soften his refined features. Peeking from that supple beard were lips so soft and full it took all of Havoc's restraint not to rip that helmet off and give them a bite. Instead, they shifted their focus to Maynard's body. Maynard looked good in the spacesuit, though he preferred a more scholarly look. His day-to-day outfits were a balance of smart and comfortable. The way the tortoiseshell frame of his glasses complemented his copper-colored eyes was stunning, and Havoc wanted a closer look at them.

He let out a wolf-whistle directed at his boyfriend.

"Shit—" Maynard bumped his helmet on the bottom of a desk. "Havoc! Go back to your wing!"

"There is nothing there to see but some tacky group photos. I got bored, so I thought I'd check on you."

"Photos?" Maynard stood. "Let me see."

"Later," Havoc seated themself atop a desk. "Tell me, is he everything Lochlan boasted he would be?" Maynard turned his attention back to his scanner, the other love of his life. "Hellooo?"

"What are you talking about?" Maynard sighed.

"How much did you see? We know Lochlan's easy—an especially curvaceous plastic bag could seduce him—but I'll admit he's got a winning streak for lookers. If he was so keen to marry, then Vince must be exceptionally hot. So what does he have?"

Maynard went to tug on the collar of a shirt that was not there. "I saw nothing."

"Two dicks? A forked tongue?"

Maynard looked ready to hide under a desk as Havoc continued his intense stare. "He's...he has a nice figure; surprisingly sculpted and tattooed."

"Tattooed...." Havoc winked at Maynard. "Well, I can certainly see the appeal."

"It's impossible to imagine he was ever a priest." Maynard's already brick-red face deepened a shade further. "Lord, I'll never be able to look him in the eye again."

Havoc snickered. "It is *adorable* how shy you are at your age."

"It's not shyness. It's..."

"Annoyance."

"No."

"Disdain?"

"No."

"You're not thinking of opening our relationship, are you?"

"No! I'm just getting to know him at my own pace."

"What's that? Zero kilometers per hour?"

Maynard glowered at them. "You must be having a harder time than I am, surely."

"On the contrary! Me and Vince have all kinds of fun. When the heavenly Father graces me with his presence, we love to play whack-a-mole. He's the mole." Showing all of their teeth, Havoc grinned.

Maynard shook his head. "Please don't scare him off."

"I can't help it! He's so jumpy! Just like you when we first met. It takes me back...." Havoc released a wistful sigh, swept up in the nostalgia of a younger Maynard. He was so precious, bumbling over his words and trembling at the thought of holding Havoc's hand. Horrified, but delighted by every monstrous form Havoc could take.

Surfacing from those loving memories, Havoc opened their eyes to see Maynard glaring again. "Jealous, starlight?"

"I won't be able to do much for you if Lochlan actually gets mad."

Havoc waved Maynard off. "Oh, Lochlan will be fine. He always bounces back after his little flings. I'm just having some fun before the carnage."

Maynard shook his head and made way for the next chamber. He held out his hand, inviting Havoc to join him. "It wouldn't kill you to be nicer."

Havoc leapt off the desk, striding past Maynard as he prodded, "At least I don't hole up in the lab all day pretending he doesn't exist."

Maynard clicked his teeth. He opened his mouth to defend himself, but tripped over a loose panel on the floor and stumbled into the door ahead of them. With a hollow clang, his scanner collided with the gate. In response, a forceful thud resounded from the opposite side, followed by the rippling screech of something unnatural. Shock rendered the couple silent as they stared at each other, wide-eyed.

Maynard's gaze flared with curiosity. He reviewed the keypad, entering the same passcode they used for every other gate. "This lock has been overridden. I can't open it."

Havoc squinted. "And *why* are we trying to get in there?"

"We need Lochlan." Maynard spun on his heel and marched away from the door. Havoc, knowing the captain's process, forwent asking for an explanation and chased behind.

❖✦❖

They ventured to the east wing and found Lochlan in the second chamber—having learned his lesson—talking on his comm, off the open channel.

Havoc scoffed at Vince's projected image. "Gods, is he really calling you again?" Lochlan flinched at Havoc's sudden voice over the broadcast. "Doesn't he have any hobbies?"

Muted, Lochlan muttered something, then stared at his comm in confused frustration. It seemed Vince had hung up. Lochlan returned to the open channel to huff out, "Where did you come from?"

"I'll give you one guess." Havoc pointed a thumb behind them to the opposite end of the hall.

"Did you come here just to bug me or what?"

"I'm cutting exploration time now. Follow me," Maynard said, turning back toward the west wing.

"Me first." Lochlan grabbed hold of Maynard's suit. "Are you seeing this?" He gestured to the surrounding chamber.

Havoc glanced about. Their jaw hung open, unease settling in their stomach—this time, not because of the snacks. In the center of deep space, aboard what was essentially a glorified ambulance, the crew found themselves inside what appeared to be an artillery bunker.

A Totally Normal Amount of Blasters

Chapter 05

//Maynard

"What the hell is all of this?" Maynard asked, picking up a blaster the size and weight of a border collie.

"It's not a first-aid kit," Lochlan answered.

Self-defense measures aboard any space craft were a must; this was just overkill. Lochlan's round of exploration had landed him in an area dedicated to storage. Basic medical supplies filled the first chamber; harmless so long as you didn't find yourself on the receiving end of one but the supplies in this chamber more closely resembled those found in Maynard's tech workshop than what one would expect to see in a doctor's office.

Maynard turned his attention to Havoc, who was looking around the room with their eyes glowing. "Anything else we should know about?"

"Nothing stands out." Havoc opened a random jar and sniffed it. They seemed a bit disappointed to be reminded that a pane of glass separated them. "It's mostly labels. That's the escape pod, in case that wasn't obvious." They pointed at a quick-access door with no lock and an exit sign above it; a glowing green escape pod logo. Maynard noted the oddity of the pod remaining in place. He thought it probable the station's crew possessed a shuttle but, in an asteroid collision and hull breach, the escape pod would have been the faster and far safer option in an emergency.

"Okay, then," he puffed. "Maybe this goes without saying, but they're definitely hiding something. This might have to do with what we found. Come on." Maynard didn't make it far, stopping when he recognized a collection of out-of-place machines.

One device in particular caught his eye. Bulky and gray, the machine stood just short of him on wheels. The laser nozzle and keypad were giveaways. He checked the safety label's universal translation for confirmation.

Just as he suspected. A quantum tunneling device.

He'd never worked with one personally, only seen it collecting dust in the lab spaces of experimental physicists. What purpose could that serve here?

"Everything alright?" Lochlan asked.

Maynard was not yet sure how to answer that. "Havoc, what did you find during your exploration?"

"Oh, yes!" Havoc buzzed. "I found ice cream, this photo of the researchers, and this journal—which I opened without a key, by the way." Havoc held the book up to show it off.

Maynard was eager to examine the discoveries, in addition to enjoying the ice cream. "Excellent job, dear." He took the photo in one hand and placed the other at the small of his partner's back.

"Why, thank you, starlight. If you must know, I brilliantly fortified the keratin in my nail to—"

Lochlan snatched the journal. "So what's in it, anyway?" He pinched a corner and shook it open as if something might fall out.

"I'm in the middle of a harrowing tale here!" Havoc lunged for the book. Lochlan held the journal high, taking advantage of their height difference. Seizing the oxygen tube near the base of Lochlan's helmet, Havoc sprang onto his chest. A taunting laugh burst from Lochlan as they wrestled over the journal.

Maynard's heart rate spiked when they nearly tore the cover off. "Both of you, be careful!" He snatched the book, and Havoc's weight sent Lochlan crashing to the ground. "Good lord!"

"I'm fine, thanks," said Lochlan to the ceiling.

Havoc crossed their legs, seated upon Lochlan's chest. "To answer your question, oaf, I sort of skimmed it. From what I can tell, it's the diary of a patient. It starts out fairly legible and then it gets a little *Hamlet* toward the end."

Maynard scratched his chin. It was a small station. Bringing a patient aboard wasn't standard protocol, much less transporting them so far from their homeworld.

He squinted at the photograph. "Wait, the keypad registered six individual signatures, but there are only five people in this photo."

Havoc let out a surprised hum. "There are six bunks as well. I found this under one of them."

"The sixth person to access the keypad must have been the patient. It seems odd to provide a patient with access privileges."

Lochlan sat, sending Havoc sliding off him. "Maybe they stole it."

"Why do you say that?" Maynard asked. Lochlan gestured to the entire east wing and its hostile aura. Maynard nodded. Even he could ask a silly question now and then. "I've seen this device before. When I was working with Echelon, it was—" The ring of Lochlan's comm cut Maynard off. He grimaced at the contact screen. Maynard pinched the bridge of his nose, his fading headache returning to sharp focus. "If that is Vincent again, please make him aware that I am confiscating your comm."

"No phones in class?" Lochlan received a scowl in response. "Relax, I got this." He stepped back into the previous chamber and answered the call. "Vino, listen—"

Before Lochlan could get a word out, Vincent was on the offensive. The usual slow, lilting tone came in quick and hot. Lochlan remembered to remove his comm from the open channel but did not remember to do so with himself. The distance prevented Maynard from hearing the other side of the conversation.

"What are you talking about?" Lochlan allowed Vincent to speak. "I'm in the middle of something here." He paused again. "What do you want from me? I called you the second we landed. You asked me to call you in a few hours, I told you I was gonna call in a few hours—you're not even giving me a chance to—alright, I don't want to be a dick, but you're acting—" The call ended. "Well, 'good night' to you too."

"Wow. That went really well." Havoc gave a small, quick clap. "No, I mean it. You really showed him!"

"'Good night'?" Maynard consulted his watch. It was still early in the afternoon.

"Guess he's done talking to me. Well fine! Now I can get some real work done!" In a tantrum, Lochlan stormed past the crew.

"What a shame," Havoc mocked.

Maynard rummaged through his bag again in search of anything to relieve his pressing headache. It felt like the right time to have 'the talk,' and he wanted to be in the right mindset before advising Lochlan of his idiocy.

"Be honest. Am I being a jackass?"

"Is it really any surprise that Vince is the obsessive type?" Havoc asked. "He married you after a week of knowing you."

"Darling, don't be unfair." Maynard zipped his bag, finding no remedy for his headache. "It was twelve weeks. You and Vincent can talk it out when we get back." *Let that be soon.*

Although he wanted to help his friend, Maynard worried about the repercussions of his own 'advice.' It was anyone's guess what he would say. One thing was certain: he had a tendency to rub one's nose in it.

It was a still morning, some months back when Lexie—Kaelith? No, it was definitely Elias....

The person's identity escaped Maynard. Their leaving mattered. A shouted curse and a half-dressed sprint through the living room marked the end of Lochlan's typical one-night-stand routine.

Maynard remained seated on the couch, eyes glued to his newspaper. "Lochlan...."

"*Don't* be an asshole," Lochlan, clad in only boxers, grumbled from the kitchen island.

Maynard hummed. "Does it make me an asshole if I say 'I told you so'?"

"Yes."

"Then I won't. I'll just say...I was right and you were wrong." Maynard shrugged.

"You're always fucking right." Lochlan sat on the couch. The impact of his plop caused the seat to bounce and Maynard's coffee to spill.

Maynard shook the dribble off his hand, splattering Lochlan. "You know what else I'm right about? Now we have to shop at a different grocery store because I can't make eye contact with the cashier."

"I really liked them...." Lochlan sank into the seat.

Maynard put his dripping mug down. "Sure you did."

"Well. I was working my way to like." Lochlan swiped the drink and downed the rest of it.

Maynard stood and threw the newspaper in Lochlan's lap, heading for the kitchen. "Find us a new grocery store. One I don't have to wear headphones in. And to be absolutely *clear*, I said 'grocery store,' not brothel."

"Thanks, Pierce. You always know what to say."

"Remember that I love you." Maynard poured himself a fresh cup of coffee. "Remind yourself while you look for a new grocery store."

"Yeah, yeah."

The morning's tension dissipated quickly. By the afternoon, they had forgotten all about the incident and were back to being friends. As if it had never even happened. Maynard sensed that things with Vincent would not be so simple.

He listened in on many arguments between his best friend and those who courted him. To call Lochlan an idiot and tell him to leave someone came easily. Obviously, marriage would make things far more complicated. For matters of the heart, Maynard was completely out of his depth, unable to offer sensible advice. To be frank, his own relationship was beyond his capabilities. This situation was best left alone; the crew had more pressing matters.

"I want to show you what we found." Maynard handed the journal back to Havoc. "Translate this."

"The *whole* thing?"

"Yes, the whole thing."

Havoc cleared their throat and began their dramatic retelling of the diary's events. As Havoc read, Maynard guided the crew through the chambers back toward the research and clinical laboratories.

The passages chronicled the onboard experience of Xijax, a young man with a memory condition brought on by a work injury. Depressed after years of struggling to find a doctor who would offer him more advice than 'rest,' he moved from Alqen, a planet bordering the Milky Way and Kratos galaxies, to the upper west quarter-sphere of Corvora to join Corvora Mercy Hospital's Retro-cognition Clinical Trial. Dr. F'vr and Dr. Harris, the lead researchers, carried out comprehensive memory testing. Xijax showed improvement; then, inexplicably, post-surgery he was in a state of constant fatigue, hunger, and irritability. Cut off from home and everyone he knew, his memories slowly slipped away. It took many painful days before he asked to withdraw from the trial.

"The next part is all drawings. Do you want me to describe them?" Havoc asked.

"Let me see." Lochlan took the journal.

"Okay, good, because I wouldn't know where to begin. It's a mess. The line work is garbage," Havoc said. Maynard glowered at them. "Oh right! Start with something positive.... Well, his use of color is quite unique, actually. It really conveys a downward spiral."

Lochlan tossed the book to Maynard. "Hawk is right. It's dog shit. I can't make heads or tails of this."

"Can you two please be a bit more respectful?"

"I don't know, *can* I?" Lochlan and Havoc asked in unison. Overjoyed by the opportunity to turn one of Maynard's favorite grammar traps back on him, they gave each other a high-five.

"Grow up," Maynard huffed.

Featured on the next few pages were drawings. Maynard could only guess that the first image was a self-portrait. Xijax covered his face in black pen scribbles and then adorned it with stars.

The following page depicted a night sky. The same drawing covered the next thirty-plus pages: a large, multi-colored spiral. Lastly, another image of the night sky. Maynard handed the book back to Havoc to continue reading.

"'Day 14. I told Dr. Harris that I can't do this anymore. It's too painful. She's taking me back to Corvora tomorrow.'" Havoc flipped to the last page. "In fittingly horrific penmanship, it says, 'Called for help.' Nothing more." Havoc clapped the journal shut and took a bow. "Et scène."

Lochlan shot a look of concern. "There's a nexus not too far from here. Six months and no one spotted the SOS?"

"I check the radar every day and didn't catch a glimpse of the beacon until we were hovering within range for the better part of a week," Maynard said. "And that's not even the strangest item on our list. As I was saying—before being so rudely interrupted—" Maynard glared at Lochlan like a teacher would at a disruptive student. Lochlan responded by giving the middle finger. How characteristically childish of him. With an eye roll, Maynard returned the bird and carried on. "I saw a quantum tunneling device in the other chamber. I am not sure what it's doing here, but I have a sneaking suspicion this isn't a sanctioned medical research center."

"You think the hospital is up to something?" Lochlan asked.

"Could be. We won't know until we get into this room." Maynard stopped in front of the last chamber in the wing. "The previous passcode hasn't worked on this keypad. A good shock should fry the mechanism. I was waiting to bring you over here on account of the—"

As if on cue, a powerful bang resounded from the opposite side of the door along with a guttural shriek.

Lochlan leapt in front of and threw an arm over both his companions. When the banging ceased, he released his arms into an agitated shake. "Jesus, Pierce, you want to lead with that next time?"

"It's very secure." Maynard knocked on the door twice. The other side responded violently, thrashing against the metal and causing the lights to flicker. Maynard moved out of the way of the falling wall fixture. "Seems it doesn't like it when you tap the glass," he chortled. The crew booed him. He clicked his teeth. "I just don't understand you two. This is the fun part! Exploration, discovery—"

"What's behind the door?" Lochlan and Havoc shouted together.

Maynard flinched at the wall of sound. He shook his head and pulled his raygun from its holster. It should suffice as their key. "Well, there is only one way to find out." Maynard approached the lock. "Are we ready?"

Havoc and Lochlan exchanged nods. Together, they gave him the "Ready," committed to braving whatever lay beyond the gate.

Maynard pulled the trigger. A concentrated bullet of electric blue energy swarmed the lock.

Once the shock settled, the unlatch rang throughout the empty hall; dull grating followed a metallic clack. With a hiss, the pressure escaped and the door nudged open.

No one spoke. An uncanny clicking echoed from beyond the door. It sounded curious. The sound grew louder, as if it were approaching the door to investigate.

Maynard held his breath as long, spindly gray fingers wrapped around the edge of the threshold. Dark wispy tendrils of some unrecognizable energy seeped through the crack. Something slowly pushed open the entrance.

Spiraling
Chapter 06

//Lochlan

Whatever this was, it was unlike anything Lochlan had ever seen. A dusty figure, like a shadow, emerged from behind the door. When it reached out with its gangling arms, its skin and tendons were so thin that the station lights shone through. It had no mouth, no eyes, just two sharp horns and a dark spinning vortex where its face should be.

One narrow foot in front of the other, it approached the crew. Lochlan's body acted on its own. He ushered them backward. This creature was no animal, no sentient. It was a monster. Hopefully, it was a friendly one, but he wasn't about to take the chance.

He checked on Maynard and Havoc, both studying it in their own ways. Havoc's glowing eyes expanded. They were running through their 'memory' of different living things. "I've got nothing," they said, crouching further behind Lochlan.

"Okay, then..." Maynard tapped his comm. He lowered his voice as he spoke into it. "Log #690—"

Un-fucking-believeable. Lochlan nudged him. "Oh, so when *I'm* on the phone it's distracting, but *you*—"

"*Phone*? Did they just thaw you out of ice?" Havoc was about to receive an elbow to their ribs when they clocked Maynard chewing his lips. He had something to say. Clearly. "Maynard Ambrose Percival, don't you dare."

The words shout out of Maynard's mouth like arrows. "Actually, the word telephone comes from the Greek 'tele' meaning far and 'phone' meaning voice. The etymology suggests that you could consider anything that allows users to conduct a conversation from afar as a 'telephone'. And, technically speaking, we consider a device a telephone so long as it converts sound into electronic signals. Which a comm does."

"Ha!" Lochlan pointed at them. "That makes you double wrong, dickhead!" Every time their voices raised, the creature tipped its head.

"Hush!" Maynard got back on his comm. "Beyond the door was a creature of...indiscernible genus. It is approaching us now, which is why we are speaking *quietly*." He pointed a frown at his crew. "So far, the creature seems...calmer than expected...." Maynard squeezed Lochlan's shoulder, a signal that he would step out from behind. Lochlan knew better than to try stopping him. It was like trying to stop the sun from rising.

"Of fucking course." Havoc muttered under their breath. "Pace yourself, pervert."

Maynard held a hand out to the beast, palm open. It hunched into a crouch and approached with its head lurched.

Lochlan felt a clamp on his arm. Looking down, he saw Havoc with their usual aloof face, but their iron-clad grip on his wrist told a different story. All went silent, breaths held as Maynard's fingertips were just centimeters away from contact.

Lochlan's comm went off.

The sharp ping startled everyone, monster included.

"What the hell?" Lochlan stared at his comm in total confusion. In an instant, dozens of missed call alerts and text messages flooded in.

"Shut that off!" Havoc scrambled for the mute button. The creature shook its head, seeming more and more pissed off with each chime.

With a screech, it swatted Maynard's hand away. The suction of the creature's whirling body frayed the fabric from his glove. "Shit! Don't let it touch you!"

The crew hollered as the creature lunged toward them. Lochlan shoved Havoc out of the way, narrowly avoiding being tackled. "Okay, no more petting the monsters. We need to have a serious talk about survival instincts, Pierce!"

Maynard found an instant patch in his bag and slapped the sticky foil over his fingers, sealing the hole. "Oh? I'm sure this will go about as well as your talk with Vincent." He drew his gun. A bullet struck the creature's chest, blowing it backward.

It flipped over and began crawling its way to Havoc. "He means poorly." They removed their glove to morph their arm into a tentacle, grabbed hold of a support beam on the opposite side of the chamber, and yanked themself away.

The creature turned toward Lochlan again. "I know what he means!" He dodged another lunge.

"But do you understand?" Maynard continued to blast from a distance. He hit the creature square in the face, but it vacuumed up the blast, unfazed.

"Well, what's that supposed to mean?" Lochlan asked. Of all the times to get abstract, it wasn't now.

"It means you're a pigheaded idiot and you don't listen to anyone!" Havoc positioned themself on the ceiling to get a good view of the creature. "Just admit you've been conned."

Lochlan rolled his eyes. "Are we really having this talk right now?" He continued to throw whatever he could find.

"If not now, then when?" Maynard asked. "We could die here!"

"Not helping!" Havoc and Lochlan shouted.

"Well, I refuse to without trying to talk some sense into you one last time!" Maynard dodged a shelf being thrown his way.

While the creature faced away from him, Lochlan cracked a chair over its head. "Fine! Just come out with it, then!" He guessed he shouldn't deny the last words of a dying man.

Maynard ducked behind a desk. "You married a total stranger!"

"He's not a stranger!"

"The man is nothing like you described." Havoc's eyes flashed as they studied the creature. "Sensitive hearing. But lots of blind spots! It can only see straight ahead of itself."

Maynard peeked out from his shelter to lob a smoke bomb toward the creature. Lochlan maneuvered around the smoke and slid behind the desk.

He had described Vince to his friends exactly as he knew him, but they hadn't given Vince the chance to show that sweet, fun-loving side of himself. "Can you blame the guy for being nervous? We got married and the next morning he was in space! He's never even left the planet!" That stupid journal and its crappy drawings got Lochlan thinking about how unsettling it must be to be swept away from everything you've ever known to live with a bunch of grouchy old fucks in a floating metal death trap. "Damn it." And somehow Lochlan had convinced himself that it was 'romantic.' He really regretted fussing at Vince on the call earlier. "I threw him to the wolves. In case nobody ever told either of you, you're not friendly dogs."

"I resent that! I'm delightful!" Havoc dropped into the hiding place alongside the crew and lowered their voice. "But...maybe you have a point about May." Havoc's boyfriend scowled at them. "Sorry, my star. You're more like the dog at the park that was never properly socialized."

Lochlan whispered, "You just sit by the fence waiting to be let out instead of playing with the other dogs."

Maynard's eyes rolled. "Okay, fine. Let's forget that Havoc has actually gotten rabies before, but let's not brush aside the fact that your relationship moved way too quickly!"

The smoke dissipated, and the creature scanned the room for the trio.

"Yeah, what happened to 'long distance'?" Havoc asked.

"I told you already! He asked to come along and I couldn't say no! I didn't want to be apart either!"

"You could have stopped at asking him to move in. That would have been absurd enough, but easy to clean up," Maynard said. "But asking him to marry you? Lochlan, this is easily the stupidest thing you've ever done!"

Lochlan groaned, "It just came out of me! When you know, you know!"

The creature had spotted them; the crew needed to keep moving. "We need a better plan," Maynard sighed.

Lochlan thought for a second. What the crew needed was time. If he could push the creature back into the room it came from, they could use the fail-safe lock to keep it in place for now. Lochlan sprang over the desk with a grunt. He whistled at Maynard, eyeing the chamber.

Maynard gestured with his head, ordering Lochlan to head inside, then fired another blast at the creature to pull its attention to him. "So that's it? You 'knew' and that's all it takes?" He continued, crushing Lochlan's wish that he'd lost track of the conversation.

Havoc slipped into the creature's blind spot while Lochlan ran into a mangled operating room. The thing must have been stuck in here for a while; if the rest of the station was a thunderstorm, this chamber looked like a tornado hit it. Feeling better about his plan, Lochlan looked for something to lure the creature back inside.

He threw around the contents of the shelves and shouted into the other room, "Well, professor, since you know every damn thing, why don't you tell me how you knew that the cult leader who was trying to murder us was the one?!"

"That's different!" The couple retorted.

"'Cult leader' is a little dramatic," Havoc added.

Hearing Havoc's voice from behind it, the creature turned toward them and away from the operating room.

Havoc turned into slime. Without a skeleton, the suit was like a rag doll, letting him dodge attacks.

"You called it 'the Order of the Only One,' you lunatic. You called your followers the 'chosen'."

"Don't the Choristers believe Vince is 'chosen'? Is that why he's so willing to follow others around blindly?" Havoc mocked.

Lochlan brushed off the nagging feeling that Havoc might have a point and noticed the operating table was on wheels. It was better than nothing. "You know what? It is different!" He gripped the table and charged forward. "At least Vince has never tried to rip my eyes out! So, in my book, my relationship's got a leg up on yours!" He burst from the room, careening toward the creature.

"This isn't about us!" Maynard swept in to pull his partner out of the path just in time for Lochlan to ram into the creature, knocking it over. "Look at you two today; this is clearly not what he expected."

The creature stood back up with ease. Seething, Lochlan made a u-turn and knocked into it again. It clung to the table as he pushed it back into the operating room. Once inside, he used the full force of his weight and increased output to his leg to pin the creature against the wall.

Maynard whistled to get Lochlan's attention and pointed toward a tall metal supply shelf bolted to the wall. Lochlan understood. He slammed into the creature's gut once again. When it keeled over in pain, he took the chance to bolt for the shelf. "He knew about my job! He knew about my life! Maybe I could have laid it out a little more, so what?" The creature hobbled after him.

Maynard tossed an energy snare. An orange glowing tether entangled the creature's legs, causing it to fall over. "So what happens if he decides this isn't the life for him? Have you thought about that?"

No. Lochlan couldn't let himself think about that. No matter how determined his mind was to make him spiral, he pushed all the questions aside, trusting that he had the only answer he'd ever need; he loved Vince and Vince loved him.

As long as he knew that, he didn't need to waste time picking things apart, trying to ruin a good thing. He'd done enough of that in his life.

Lochlan focused on the shelf and the few remaining sturdy bolts fastening it to the wall. He took a heavy breath and increased the output to his cybernetic arm. The artificial muscle hummed and vibrated. He grabbed the shelf's edges; steel crumpled like aluminum in his hand. A strained growl ripped out of him, along with the fixture from the wall. The anchored bolts pulled at the corners of the wall panels. With a mighty heave, he lifted the shelf and sent it crashing down. Bottles, papers, and surgical kits scattered across the floor.

Pain surging down his spine and throbbing shoulder, he checked on the creature. The damn thing kept moving. It kind of hissed at Lochlan, wriggling wildly under the shelf like a beetle.

"If you care about Vincent, consider what he really wants," Maynard added.

Lochlan's nostrils flared. Blood, boiling and blurring his vision, fueled his stomp toward the creature. "Enough!" He used his titanium fist to bash in the creature's chest repeatedly, but it continued to squirm. "Maybe you're right! Maybe I'm crazy!" With each hit, the vibration carried to Lochlan's spine. The vacuum ripped apart his arm, the prosthetic still transmitting pain to his brain. "Maybe—" He breathed. "Maybe this isn't what Vince wants and maybe he's gonna break my heart into a million fucking pieces...." Finally, the creature stopped moving. Lochlan straightened up, his breath coming in ragged gasps. "It's him. He's the one. If it's not him, then it's nobody."

Sweat dripped from his brow. He rested a foot on the shelf and closed his eyes, concentrating on slowing his breath.

Vince meant those drunken midnight vows. "For better, for worse, in sickness and in health, to the edge of the universe and beyond." His big, watery eyes did a damn good job of making Lochlan feel like he meant it.

Lochlan caught his breath. He turned to walk away from the operating room, ready to put an end to the mission, when he noticed the creature's hand give a tiny twitch. "Oh, come on!"

Divorced Uncle Rock

Chapter 07

//Lochlan

Lochlan removed the rest of his arm and tossed the scrap to the ground. The creature was still alive but—thanks to him—barely kicking. Pinned was good enough for now. At least the crew could regroup; he was too tired to think. He dragged his heavy feet toward the exit.

Maynard directed Havoc with his eyes before making his way to the manual lock, a fail-safe for the electrical system. Havoc caught on and went after the scrap arm. They sighed as they dusted it off, "Why are you always so—"

"Are you with me or what?" Lochlan snapped.

Havoc cradled the arm to their chest, mumbling, "Do you need *everything* spelled out for you?"

After securing the lock, Maynard joined. He placed a hand on his partner's shoulder. "What Havoc is trying to say—well, what Havoc and I are trying to say.... We were just thinking that after what happened with Evelyn, I mean—I've never seen you so—"

"Miserable! You ass! It took you a *long* time to bounce back from that!"

Lochlan's heart stuttered, like he'd heard the whispers of a ghost. "Wait. This is about Ev?" He hadn't even said his ex-wife's name out loud in years. Just hearing it now made him all kinds of antsy.

He and Evelyn followed all the rules. Lochlan proposed as soon as he felt grown up enough, waited until they were 'financially prepared,' and had a nice big wedding with a hundred people he barely knew. His first marriage had all the makings of a perfect match, but Lochlan Murdock wasn't made for love. He wasn't kind, or smart, or talented at anything. He had his father's temper in a body built like a punching bag, and so that's what he did. All his life.

They'd had it out one night after a match. He really thought he was going to be the next best thing in boxing. Lochlan took on anyone and, if the money was good enough, he'd even do it out of the ring. He told himself he was doing it for her. For them.

That night should have put him in the hospital, but he walked it off. Growing up poor, doctors' visits were not exactly entertained. She begged, and it wasn't the first time either. He'd gotten so agitated with her for even suggesting it and her well of patience ran dry. "Your problem is that you don't care about anything, Lochlan. I will not sit here and watch you kill yourself. If you don't care enough about me to know that this is killing me too, then I have nothing more to say to you." And she was gone. Too proud to even take her things with her. He couldn't even blame her. She had every right to be angry.

The night Evelyn left replayed in his mind like a broken tape stuck in a VCR for years. It distorted over time and faded with work and good company. Just crept up on him whenever he was alone, so he got very good at never being alone. At one time, she was his best friend. Now, they were like strangers. Every time he brought someone new to bed, he reminded himself that every fling started as a stranger and it wouldn't hurt to keep it that way. For years, Lochlan Murdock belonged to no one.

Until Vince.

Lochlan wasn't a *total* idiot. He knew what it looked like from the outside. But how could he help himself? From the moment they met, being with Vince felt like being with another part of himself. It was just embarrassing the way he'd wake up early, get dressed, and wait outside for the mail truck, pretending it was 'just a coincidence' that he was outside every day. He would have been happy just to have Vince as a friend, a pretty face giving him attention. *This* was beyond Lochlan's wildest dreams. Vince charged right into his life.

Nothing about him should have made sense to Lochlan. He was a sensitive soul with a condition that punished him for feeling anything and a bone to pick with the same Gods he felt fiercely loyal to. But it did make sense. He was like Lochlan, always fighting with himself and trying to be a decent person anyway. If Lochlan ruined everything he touched, Vince turned it into gold. No one had ever been so tender or understanding and, as much as Lochlan tried to deny his feelings, he didn't last long.

Maynard kneaded the patch on his glove. "You haven't seriously dated anyone in years. You've been—"

"Fucking around! And just when I've accepted that you're going to die young from some venereal disease, you bring this mail-order bride home and you expect us to believe that you're not having some sort of episode?" Maybe it was exhaustion but Havoc's tone was unusually serious. "I wanted to test you for dementia!"

"We're just looking out for you."

Awkward silence hung between the three of them, all with eyes on the floor. Feelings were not something any of them had the luxury of expressing in their past lives. Anger was the only thing that came naturally. They survived all these years together by screaming at each other, trusting that anything said would be forgiven then forgotten.

Lochlan pushed the air from his nose. "Fair enough." He looked them both in the eyes as he said, "But I mean it. It's different this time."

Maynard stared at Havoc, softened gaze broadcasting that he was somewhere far away. "Oh, who am I to judge? If you say it's different, then we'll believe you."

"Speak for yourself!" Havoc was nudged. They shifted around, silent for a moment before mumbling, "You're not allowed to retire."

Lochlan raised a brow. "What are you talking about?"

"If Father Luque decides this isn't the life for him, you're not allowed to retire. You signed up for this. You can't just back out and leave all the work to me and May." A wavering frown and bouncing leg said everything that Havoc never would.

Lochlan smirked. "I'm not going anywhere."

"Good. Well. We are getting the hell out of here at least!" Havoc made a sharp turn for the exit.

"My love, we still need to investigate the cockpit."

The crew headed back to the north wing where the cockpit was. The one chamber ahead of it was empty aside from a few built in benches.

"I'm so tired," Havoc whined.

"Almost there, darling. Lochlan has already investigated this room so we shouldn't be long." Maynard entered the passcode into the keypad. On the door sliding open, something pressed up against the other side fell forward. A lifeless body toppled onto the ground, forcing everyone to jump back.

The captain stared at Lochlan with wide eyes. Lochlan raised his arm. "I swear to God, I didn't see that earlier."

Maynard looked inside the room. "No wonder. This is a storage area between the center chamber and the cockpit." Lochlan used his foot to flip the corpse over. Realizing now how badly he'd fucked up his spine, he hissed at a twinge in his lower back. "Are you alright?"

"I'm fine." Lochlan leaned against Havoc. "My guess is the poor guy tried to run and didn't make it."

"The name tag says F'vr." Havoc pointed to Maynard's bag where the photo and journal were. "He's one of the lead researchers."

A sudden onslaught of pings and vibrations hit the crew's ears. "Uhhh...." Maynard showed the crew his comm. Dozens of missed calls. Havoc wrinkled their nose at their own comm with the same 'mailbox full' alert.

"Shit! Vince!" Aiming for his forehead, Lochlan hit the glass of his helmet instead. The comm on his cybernetic arm had become dust in the wind.

"That can't be right...." Maynard wiped the screen. "What day is it?"

Havoc blinked like something was wrong with their eyes. "It's March 28th. Isn't it?"

"Yeah?" Lochlan's brow turned up. Havoc showed him their lock screen. Above an unflattering picture of Maynard's nostrils, the date April 9th displayed. Lochlan squinted at the screen. "What the hell? That's like, a week off."

"It's closer to two weeks," Maynard corrected.

"Very good, starlight. That's what we were concerned with."

"Gimme that!" Lochlan yanked Havoc by the wrist and used their comm to call Vince.

"I didn't hear a 'please'!"

Vince answered the call before the first ring finished. He came into the picture, filtered through a gloomy aurora. His hair was a mess, caked makeup streaming down his cheeks. "Lochlan?!" He prayed in Spanish. All Lochlan could make out through the rush was a 'thank you' and 'blessings'.

"Vinni, what's wrong?" Lochlan squeezed Havoc's arm, forcing them to keep their arm up.

"*What's wrong*?! I thought you were...." Vince clearly didn't want to finish that sentence. "You're okay," he sighed. To calm down, Vince normally took four deep breaths, counting to four with each. The 4/4 count was a Chorister practice. Vince made it one breath in before the magical aurora around him condensed into embers that flashed across his face, almost singeing his hair. "Where the hell have you been?!"

"Okay, hold on! Something's up I think." Lochlan eyed the crew. Havoc's uptight face offered no answers, as clueless as Lochlan.

Thankfully, Maynard cut in. "Vincent. What day and time is it?"

"It's...April 9th, it's almost eleven o'clock. What is going on?!"

Maynard looked away, chewing his top lip. He hated speaking before confirming the facts, but he would have to this time.

"Come on, man, say something!" Lochlan dragged Maynard into the frame.

"W-well, I really can't say anything for certain...but it seems we've run into some sort of time anomaly?" Maynard wasn't sure how to hold his face, but everyone else shared an expression of total confusion. "Vincent, as far as the three of us are aware, we've only been gone for an hour. Maybe an hour and a half?"

"Wait, what? What are you talking about?" The embers around Vince died down, small sparks, and an aurora joining them. Lochlan also felt all over the place.

"I'm guessing that for you, we've been gone for almost two weeks. Is that right?" Everyone gasped.

"*Two weeks*?" Lochlan asked. "We're in a different time than Vince?"

"We were. It seems we're aligned at this moment." Maynard gasped, appearing to have a breakthrough. "Our communications have been out of sync! We've only just now received your calls."

Havoc grimaced. "So...when we thought Vince was calling you every five minutes...?"

Lochlan finally recognized just how badly he had fucked up. "Vinni, about what I said earlier, I had no idea. I swear."

The light around Vince dispelled but his expression remained irate. "Is everything okay now? Are you okay?"

Lochlan glanced at his torn up arm. He'd made it a point to keep it out of frame. "I'm okay."

"Then that's all I care about. But when you get back, we need to talk."

Lochlan's chest tightened. "Yeah." A talk. He was great at those.

Havoc cleared his throat. "While I am enjoying being the vessel for your relationship drama, my ice cream's melting."

"Keep your pants on!" Lochlan barked.

Maynard stepped between the two of them. "Let's leave now."

"Vinni, I know this sucks but I have to go and I promise you we're leaving right now. Twenty minutes."

"Twenty minutes and not a *second* over."

As the call ended, Lochlan's face crumpled. A whispered "Oof" came from Havoc.

"That...well. What to say about that?" Maynard put his fist into his hand. "It seems we've been a bit harsh."

Lochlan sighed the deepest sigh he'd ever sighed in his life. "I am in such deep shit right now..." He side-eyed Havoc. "Alright, go on. Get it out of your system."

Havoc gasped. "I could *never* kick a man while he's down!" They nudged the scrap of Lochlan's arm into his side. "But I could shoulder him!" Their audience gave them no laughter. They tapped the shoulder piece twice and mumbled into it, "Is this thing on?"

Lochlan stared out. He wasn't a religious man but, if some divine power wanted to prove their stuff by striking him down right now he'd be fine with that.

"We should hurry." Maynard held out his hand.

Lochlan groaned, surrendering the shuttle keys. *Great.* Now he had to risk the other love of his life to Maynard's shitty flying. "Hawk, set my timer for me."

"I don't take orders from you!"

"I'm disabled! Don't be a prick."

Havoc rolled their eyes and shoved the scraps into their bag. "This is what we are talking about! Lochlan sticks himself into anything with a hole and then he makes it everyone else's problem." They opened their comm. "I *cannot* keep being the glue that—uh oh," Havoc's comm was ringing. "For you, I assume."

A cold sweat prickled Lochlan's neck. "Don't tell me—" He let out a sigh of relief, noticing the time hadn't jumped. He hit the answer button. "Hey Vinni, I swear we're leaving right now."

A quick cleanup, and Vince's hair and makeup were perfect again. "Can I talk to you alone?"

Lochlan held out his hand to Havoc. "What's the magic word?" they sang.

"Gimme." He opened and closed his hand twice in an exaggerated grab.

Havoc pulled the comm from their wrist. "Try not to crush this one. Lout."

"And get your channels right," Maynard grumbled.

Lochlan stepped to the side. After triple checking the channels, he asked, "What's up?"

"I need a favor...and before you say no, remember that you owe me!"

Dishing It Out
Chapter 08

//Havoc

Finally, some fresh air. With the shuttle's oxygen generator activated, Havoc could remove their helmet. Released from their constraints, long, glossy locks sprung back to their original length.

"My side of the bed is yours, if you prefer not sleeping on the couch," Havoc said to Lochlan, although he found the mental image of wispy Vince in that enormous bed by himself and giant Lochlan smothering their tiny couch quite amusing.

A sharp "No," left Maynard as he sat upright in the pilot's seat, with a white-knuckled grip on the controls. Piloting made him so anxious, but they had no choice as Havoc was not even permitted to try. "Lochlan and I will *never* share a bed again."

Lochlan thwapped him on the shoulder. "It's not that bad!" It was. Some missions forced the crew off Leviathan's Luck for days at a time, and in the early days when funds were tight, the captain forced everyone into a single tiny hotel room together. Maynard and Havoc nearly wept with joy the first time a client offered to cover their rooms, and they forced Lochlan out.

"It's like sleeping next to a jet engine." Maynard used the knuckle of his thumb to massage his temple.

"A jet engine would be less loud."

"Damn...that's what Vinni said. He's making me stick a magnet up my nose. It actually works pretty well."

Maynard opened his mouth to speak, but then shook his head. He must have felt awful, headache defeating his relentless curiosity.

"If you picked your nose, wouldn't your finger get stuck?" Havoc asked, tapping Lochlan's metal shoulder.

Lochlan scowled toward the back seat. "I'm a grown man. I don't pick my nose."

Havoc brought a hand to their chest. "Oh, I'm *sorry*! I did not realize you were so far above the rest of us! No advanced being, such as yourself, could *degrade* himself by complying with the most barbaric of demands. Clean nostrils? What a *fool* I am to believe that *the* Lochlan Murdock, of all people, could—"

"Havoc, please!"

"Fine! It got stuck!"

Havoc snickered, leaning forward to kiss Maynard's throbbing forehead. "Thought so."

Lochlan's promise of a quick trip home proved true. Drained, the crew changed back into their regular clothing and headed through the Keel to the elevator.

Stepping onto the living floor, Maynard hemmed in a cough. He rubbed his throat, but the irritation would not wane. He hissed suddenly, grabbing his forehead. That headache must have been worse than Havoc thought. Maynard would likely gripe about how Havoc's pestering made it worse.

Lochlan patted him on the back. "You alright there, Pierce?"

"My throat is so dry. I haven't had enough water today." Maynard smacked his lips together, the lack of moisture apparent in the light sticky sound.

Havoc followed their partner into the kitchen to stow away their likely sopping box of ice cream sandwiches, but they weren't inside their bag. They knew they hadn't dropped them, which meant Maynard had thrown them away. Humans were so wasteful. It's no wonder their planet was just a sweaty ball of sewage and dying animals.

Lochlan sat on the stool by the island. "Coffee and booze don't cut it anymore. You're too old for that."

Maynard pulled a glass from the cabinet, chuckling. "Okay, fair point I—" He could not finish his sentence, for the soft laughter developed into a fit of coughing.

Havoc brushed it off at first, still rummaging through their bag and complaining under their breath. They looked up from their bag once they realized Maynard's arid hawking had dragged on for an alarming amount of time. In the presence of their worst nightmare, Havoc's complaints became insignificant. They shook off the stress and ran over to Maynard, understanding they had to work quickly. "How does your chest feel?" They placed a hand on Maynard's wrist to feel his heartbeat. "Does your arm hurt?" They detected no palpitations.

Maynard, unable to answer between coughs, dropped his glass, and Havoc's relief shattered along with it. "Water...water...," he cried.

Puzzled, Havoc supported their trembling partner, guiding his collapse to the ground between the shards. Maynard paled. The tissue of his once vivid complexion sank deeply into the hollows of his cheeks. As Maynard's strong features became gaunt and ghastly, Havoc's world seemed to shrink around them. His skin, like ashes, began flaking off, caught in a dark wind-like force reminiscent of the creature's power.

"Maynard?!" Havoc's vision was blurry with tears as they comforted him. "It's okay. You're going to be okay." The creature might have followed the crew home, but it was nowhere to be seen. A horrifying idea occurred to Havoc. Perhaps some sort of curse struck Maynard. The magic was way out of his depth, but staying put wasn't an option. What could he do? "Lochlan, get Vince!" Vince had to know something, and even if he hated Havoc's guts right now, the Father's good nature would allow him to abandon someone in need. Even so, Havoc would do anything for Maynard. He would get on his hands and knees and atone—Gods, he would even convert. "Tell him I'm sorry and—"

"Gotcha."

Havoc spun his head in its direction to see Vince stepping out from the hallway. With a graceful wave of his hand and a snap of his fingers, the energy dispersed. In an instant, life and moisture flooded back into Maynard's pores.

His wide eyes rolled forward. "What the fuck?!" he rasped, sitting up like he had just woken up from a nightmare.

"My star? You're okay?" Through watery eyes, Havoc scanned over the body of their boyfriend, patting him down. He appeared solid, his beautiful body completely back to normal. Maynard, still in shock, nodded.

Elation swelled in Havoc's chest before the rage took over. He glared at Vince, a smile playing on the necromancer's lips as he batted his doll-like lashes. Havoc, suddenly not so repentant, dropped Maynard to the ground like a rag doll and stormed over, ready to tear Vince to pieces. The sudden seizing of his collar made Vince wince. With all the venom they could muster, Havoc spat, "You demented, vile, fucked in the head, little *freak*!"

"Too far?" Vince squeaked.

"Too far?! That was the most horrifying moment of my life!" Havoc pulled back a fist.

Vince thrust his hands in front of himself, shouting, "Please, not my face!"

Havoc's arms unexpectedly trembled. Their heart, which had been pounding into their ears, slowed. "Gods...that was...I mean, *genuinely* terrifying...." Fear subsided into bewilderment, bewilderment into exhilaration. The rush of adrenaline was like coming down from a roller coaster. Their fingers, firm as gelatin, released Vince's shirt. Havoc stared in mystified wonder at their hands. Nothing had ever gotten a rise out of them like this. They had to admit that was...exactly the kind of prank they'd pull on someone if they could. "He looked like the Crypt Keeper!" Havoc cackled. "Oh my gods, it was disgusting!"

"H-how did you do that?" Maynard stood, tottering into a lurch. He should have been furious, but he staggered toward Vince with a starry-eyed fascination. "Was that a spell?" Maynard wiped the dust from his glasses. "You can do that on command?"

The couple crowded the magic user. Maynard, too, couldn't help but laugh along with Havoc's infectious howl. Vince gave a puzzled smile, presumably relieved that the couple was more entertained than bothered.

"I told you it would be fine," Lochlan piped in. "We thought you two earned a little torture after everything you put Vinni through."

Vince chuckled. "I'm sorry. But I wasn't gonna let the snake thing *go*." A smirk passed between Havoc and him. So, Father Luque had a sick sense of humor. "It is a spell, yes. I can tell you all about it sometime—" Maynard eagerly pulled out his notebook. It was quite high praise. Havoc found it a charming trait that, when Maynard's mind was in high gear, he favored the gripping connection of hand writing. Vince, taken aback by Maynard's intense enthusiasm, continued. "Or right now. Sure. My church, uh, The Radiant Choir, has these spell books called the Holy Octave. This one is from the necromancy book and—what the fuck happened to your arm?!" Vince pushed Havoc and Maynard apart to see Lochlan better.

Lochlan rose with one arm up, surrendering. "Okay, before you freak out; it's fine. Pierce is gonna build me a new one."

Maynard puffed. "Says who?"

"Says my husband, who's gonna turn us both into a pile of ash if you don't."

Vince approached Lochlan with fire trailing behind him. "What is the matter with you?!"

Lochlan retreated, using the kitchen island as a barrier. "Uh. You wouldn't hit a guy with one arm, would you?"

As Havoc watched the antics, a wild grin split his face. Here he is. Suddenly, Havoc could see the man his friend described, and this man might be worth getting to know. "Oh! Vince, let me run a joke by you. It went over these idiots' heads, but I think you'll like it. Lochlan, where is your shoulder piece?"

What'll It Cost Ya?
Chapter 09

//Lochlan

In Lochlan's opinion, everything sounded way worse than it actually was.

"You stuck your *arm* into a *vacuum*?" Magical electricity exploded around Vince, and Lochlan could swear that some of it tried to grab him.

He scratched the back of his head. "You had to be there...?"

Leviathan's Luck had moved to the War Room and—out of guilt—voted unanimously to invite Vince. Only a screen and a holoprojector sat around a white round table. Now and then, Vince shivered or wobbled on top of the metal crate he was using as a seat after insisting that the tired crew take their usual chairs.

"Are you actually insane?"

"Yes," was Maynard and Havoc's collective, ungrateful answer.

Vince covered his face. He was quiet, lights sparking and dying around him. With a telepathic agreement to leave him be, the crew exchanged tense peeks.

Lochlan understood now what Maynard was getting at. This job tested relationships. He could remember a few times when even his younger sister had chewed his ear off about taking better care of himself. Time showed her that her brother was not going to change. She saw Lochlan through many shitty gigs, and if Vince thought this was bad, he wouldn't have the stomach for Lochlan's old job.

Before Leviathan's Luck, Lochlan couldn't have found himself more desperate for cash. He wasn't about to help his sister raise a baby girl while living in his car, so he felt lucky the day Jude found him. A sour feeling in his stomach rose with bile in his dry throat, but whatever his gut was saying, Lochlan was so hungry he couldn't hear it. He started working for the crime boss that week. He couldn't bring himself to tell Joan. Not that it took her long to put two and two together.

In her manicured hands, Joan rolled together a stack of legal pamphlets. As hard as she could, she smacked Lochlan's nose with the makeshift baton and tossed a box of princess-patterned bandages into his lap. "You better not leave me to plan your funeral, jerk!" In the kitchen of his sister, Lochlan sat with his black blazer hung on a wooden chair. He tucked a bruised fist under his nose. It was already bleeding when he got there. His attempt to move the drip from the cushion to the floor just missed, staining his white button-up instead. "And if any of your hookups end up in your will, I swear to God!"

He shook the box of bandages at her. "You got any other options?"

Joan picked up Candy, her daughter, from a playmat on the ground and settled the baby onto her hip. She scowled at Lochlan. "What? You're too tough for pink now? Get over yourself." She set Candy in a high chair at the table, opened up a jar of mushy carrots, and sniffed the contents before making a face. Typically, Neil, her husband, handled this, but he was at the grocery store. When Lochlan first arrived, he was thankful for a moment of privacy. Not only because Lochlan could be a wreck in front of Joan, but because Neil was squeamish around blood. Now Lochlan wanted Neil there to hide behind.

"Fine." Lochlan pushed up the sleeves of his shirt as Joan tried to force her daughter to eat.

"They're the only ones Candy will use, so it's that or I take you to the hospital," Joan said.

"No hospitals." Lochlan had to use two bandages on each knuckle to cover them fully. "Can't afford that right now."

"Lochlan, I can-"

"No, you can't."

A blow sent the spoon from Joan's grasp. With a tiny hand, Candy pounded the high chair tray and reached for her uncle. He picked up the spoon and sent it flying toward the baby with dips, flips, and spaceship sound effects. When Candy giggled, he popped the spoon into her mouth. He looked at Joan, waiting for a thank you. She tucked a strand of long brown hair behind her ear. "Wash your hands," she sighed. He deserved that. "One day she's gonna be old enough to know that's not ketchup on your shirt. Next time Jude does something stupid, tell him to figure it out himself."

"He's my boss, Joanie. It's my job to clean up after him."

"Well, he's not my boss, so tell him." Joan stood to grab a napkin for the baby. "Or he'll have me to face."

Lochlan smiled. "I'm his bodyguard. So, you'll have me to face."

"Easy work. I point to something pretty and you'll be gone faster than that cheap toupee of his in a hurricane." The siblings shared a laugh. Joan took hold of Lochlan's hand and examined the damage. "Just...be careful, alright? You only get one body."

In the present, Lochlan looked down at his arm, where flesh once was. He wanted to tell Vince not to worry, but how?

Vince massaged his jaw. "How long is it going to take?" He pointed the question to the resident tech expert.

"Well, thankfully I have the foresight to keep some spares *on hand*," Maynard laughed. Lochlan swore he caught a twitch in Vince's eye. "Er, as you can imagine, he does this sort of thing often." It seemed Maynard chose Vince's side.

"Oh, right! *Pierce is just gonna build me a new one*," Vince said in a mocking tone, chest puffed. "You can't just blow through it and toss it into the garbage when you're done with it. It's not a condom. It's your fucking arm!"

"That's what I have been saying," Maynard added. "Well, not in those exact words...."

"Alright! Look, we've got other priorities," Lochlan grumbled. It was getting too late for this. "We have nothing, and that thing is still on the station."

"Wait, you guys are going back?" Vince's eyebrows matched the tension in his tone.

Lochlan gestured for a softer blow. Maynard understood and explained, "I'm afraid we have to. There's no telling what could happen if we leave something that dangerous unattended. We all feel like we have a responsibility to see this through." The crew nodded.

"Right...of course. I understand." The light flickering in his eyes wasn't convincing. "So, what's next?"

A doubtful look passed between the crew. "I'm beat."

"Even I need some sleep," Havoc seconded.

Maynard checked his comm. "It's past midnight. We should get some rest. We'll revisit this in the morning." He clapped, and the crew stood to break for the evening.

Before the door to their bedroom finished sliding closed, Lochlan grabbed Vince's waist and pulled him in for a kiss. He kept his forehead pressed to his husband's, not knowing where to begin. Probably with apologizing—if the thought didn't make him cringe. He kept the light off to spare Vince the sorry look on his face.

A woodsy scent drifted into the air between them when Vince fidgeted with his necklace. "Twelve days. I didn't hear from you. I didn't see you."

"I know."

"I thought you were dead. I tried summoning you from the Veil," Vince said. Lochlan couldn't stand the picture of that hopeless hunt through a literal ghost town. "You didn't show and I thought I'd lost you forever...."

Lochlan took Vince's hand and put it to his chest, rubbing small circles into the back with his thumb. "I'm right here."

"I'm glad you're home safe." With his ring finger, he wiped away a tear welling up in the corner of his eye. He shoved Lochlan and said, "But don't ever do that to me again or you'll lose the other arm," with a chuckle.

"I hear you." Lochlan wrapped his arm around Vince. In his eyes, he didn't deserve Vince's forgiveness, but it came regardless and washed over him like rain. If it were up to Lochlan, he'd never let go again. "Let's get to bed." He made too sharp a turn for the steps and hissed at an aching sensation along his spine. When he felt Vince's hand grab his arm, he bit the inside of his cheek, choosing not to worry Vince any further. "Just a little sore. Come on."

To help Lochlan climb the steps to their bed, Vince held his hand. When they arrived, Lochlan noticed several empty bottles of beer in the trash. It must have been tough falling asleep alone every night.

Lochlan tried to take his shirt off, but it got caught on a metal port sticking out of his arm. "Can I help you?" Vince asked, placing a hand on Lochlan's back.

His gut reaction was to say no, but that memory of Evelyn came back, and Lochlan couldn't shake it off. *Just this one time.* "Thanks." He held out the residual limb and allowed Vince to unhook the cloth from the small metal latch. Once he'd gotten the shirt off, Vince stood for a moment, staring blankly. "What?" Lochlan asked.

"Nothing." Vince shook his head.

Lochlan was used to the constant stares; everyone he met stared. Because it was Vince's first time seeing the dock close up, his fixated gaze made Lochlan feel a bit on edge. "Does it freak you out?"

"No." Vince smiled. "I am freaking out but not because of your arm. I'm freaking out because...it's you. I finally understand what your job is. Does that make sense?" His soft charcoal eyes peered up at Lochlan through thick lashes. *Pretty.* Lochlan nodded. Vince balled the t-shirt in his hands. "Can I touch you?"

"Go ahead." Lochlan took a seat on their bed to allow his husband an easier reach. Vince grazed Lochlan's shoulder.

The cut had been a clean one, done with surgical precision. Lochlan could at least be thankful for that. It'd been so long ago that the scarring had healed into a faint mark. Now smooth pink skin surrounded the metal implant where his prosthetic would attach.

A weird length of time passed without either of them saying anything. Lochlan cleared his throat. "So?" His husband tilted his head. Lochlan swayed nervously. "What are you thinking?"

Vince shrugged. "Really, nothing. Just that it's new. I've never seen you without something else there. Actually...I was thinking it's weird to see a part of your body without hair on it. I didn't think that was possible." Lochlan burst into laughter. Maybe it was unfair of him to expect anything else from Vince.

With a squeeze to the shoulder, Vince helped Lochlan stand and continued to undress him. He loosened the belt and undid the button on Lochlan's jeans. Lochlan caught the not-so-subtle way he took his time with the zipper.

"Hey, I know that look," Lochlan drawled, lowering his lids.

Vince smirked. "What?"

Lochlan cupped his husband's chin to tilt his face up. "You know...I'm still thinking about this morning...."

Vince's eyes rolled. "I'll remind you, again, that was actually like, forever ago."

"Yeah but, you thought about it while I was gone."

"Of course I did." Vince stood. "And I took care of myself."

"I thought we had an agreement." Lochlan said. 'Picking up where we left off' was his prime motivator for finishing the mission.

Vince stood up. "Yeah, well, that expired."

"Ouch," Lochlan winced in feigned agony. Vince gave him a consoling pat on the chest, and Lochlan pinned his husband's wrist there. "At least tell me about it."

He kept his hungry stare on Vince's lips, ignoring the comment, "It's one in the morning." An inviting rosy hue touched Vince's high cheekbones. "Fine. I waited all the way until Tuesday but I was stressed and I caught a hint of your cologne in bed, and...."

"So you thought about me?" Lochlan held his bottom lip in his teeth.

"Who else?"

The warmth in Lochlan's stomach plunged between his legs as he asked, "What'd you think about?"

Vince's hand slipped out of Lochlan's grasp, lowering and stopping just above the band of his boxers. "That time...on my lunch break when you snuck me into the base...."

"That's a pretty good one."

"Yeah...."

Vince, with eyes that burned like coal and lips slightly apart, was one sultry form Lochlan was happy to be sucked into. He reached into Vince's hair, pulling him into a passionate kiss. The arousal intensified as their kiss grew more heated.

"I missed you," Vince gasped.

"I'm gonna make it up to you—" Lochlan felt another sudden twinge in his back. He bent forward at an awkward angle to catch a spot where it didn't hurt and held his breath.

Vince held onto his shoulders, stepping back. "Are you okay?"

"I'm fine," Lochlan said, forcing the words out through a stiff sternum.

"You're...sweating."

The pang persisted. "Okay. Yeah. I'm going down," Lochlan held onto Vince as he sat himself back down on their bed.

"What's wrong?" Vince looked back and forth between the door and his comm.

"I'm just tired, sweetheart. It's nothing to worry about." Whatever spasm Lochlan was having died down enough for him to reach into his nightstand for a bottle of muscle relaxers. It completely slipped his mind to take some earlier.

"You know I'm going to worry about you no matter what, right?" Vince took a seat next to him.

Lochlan could blame it on the time. Since knowing Vince, this kind of thing just hadn't come up yet. He didn't want to admit that maybe Maynard had a point and there were parts of himself that Lochlan had glossed over. His lower jaw shifted from side to side in thought. Vince should know. "I gotta come clean about something."

"Okay?"

"It sucks to sleep with the arm and leg on," Lochlan said, wondering why it made him so nervous to.

He watched Vince's expression stay almost completely the same apart from a cocked eyebrow. "So...why do you?"

"I, uh...." Lochlan chewed his bottom lip. It wasn't shame; it was just that he'd never had a partner stick around long enough to show it to. This was his first time too.

"Not that you should *care*, but, for the record, it doesn't 'freak' me out."

"I haven't had a good night's sleep since you moved in. I'm taking the leg off tonight, so I wanted to let you know," Lochlan said. Vince nodded and let his eyes trail to the floor with a frown. "What?"

"I'm just really sorry. Of course, it's not comfortable to sleep with a big hunk of metal attached to you." Vince tapped his forehead and threw his fingers out. "I had a feeling, and I should have asked."

"I could have said something. You're not a mind reader...are you?"

Vince laughed. "No."

"Okay, good 'cause all that stuff I was thinking about you in a nun outfit was a joke."

Vince snapped his fingers. "Damn, and I was really looking forward to that."

Their soft laughs tapered. Lochlan sighed. "Old folks have a lot of ego." It wasn't Lochlan's proudest trait. Asking for help wasn't a skill he'd been born with. Despite knowing he didn't have to, he felt a need to carry himself in a certain way. To be like anyone else—maybe even better than most people. "Especially me."

"Can we both promise to speak up more?" Vince scratched Lochlan's chin.

"Promise. I'll start by telling you that you look *really* good right now."

"That's so funny. I was just thinking the same thing about you." Vince's eyes twinkled with a magical glow. "Can I help you with that?" He pointed to the leg.

"Uh." Lochlan took a fast breath. "Yeah. Sure." He scooted back and kicked his leg out. Vince knelt down. "It's going to be heavier than you think. Just grab it here and twist it out." He guided Vince's hands to a groove along his shin and pressed the release by his hip. When the engine powered off, the leg dropped heavily into Vince's hand. Vince moved with focus, but too carefully. The leg didn't budge. "You're gonna have to do it harder than that."

"You're messing with me, aren't you?" Vince teased.

"Hey. You're the one pulling *my* leg."

Vince shoved Lochlan the way he did whenever he made a 'dad joke' which only made Lochlan laugh harder. "So what do I do?" Vince laughed at himself. "It's really in there."

"Here." Lochlan scooted forward. "Step on my foot."

"Step on it?" Vince asked, like he wasn't sure he heard right.

"Yeah, just put your weight on it and I'll pop it off." He helped Lochlan stand. Although skeptical, he followed the instructions well, pressing his foot against the arch. When he did, Lochlan shouted as if Vince had stepped on bone and flesh, earning himself a smack on the arm. He held Vince's shoulder for support, rotated sharply, and heard the unlatch. The weight was off him and, damn, did his back feel better. Sitting back down, he moaned with relief.

"Good?" Vince giggled.

"The *best*." The corners of Lochlan's nerves melted away. "Drugs are kicking in nicely. Can I ask you to plug that in? Charger's in the closet." He pointed to the narrow black cabinet opposite his nightstand, which held his other mobility aids.

"Well, technically, you already asked me." Vince lifted the leg and carried it to the closet. Lochlan shot Maynard a quick thank-you text for the user-friendly design as Vince found no problem slotting into place. He crawled into bed and curled up next to Lochlan. "Gods, you weren't kidding. That thing is heavy."

As if made for it, Vince filled the crooks of Lochlan's body. Lochlan took in the soft scent of Vince's hair, cherry, spice, and a whiff of smoke.

This would have been unthinkable just a short while back. Screw his friends and whatever they thought. It was all worth it for this alone. Lochlan had never been happier in his life. He drifted off to sleep thinking Vince had never truly been a stranger to him.

Love Sucks
Chapter 10

//Maynard

Maynard chugged the last of his water and shook the cup above his mouth for its last drops. The aftereffects of Vincent's spell left him feeling parched even after a third refill. When he was sure no droplets remained, he refilled it from a matching indigo carafe placed by the reading nook on the lower level of his and Havoc's bedroom. He wiped his mouth and asked Havoc, "Are you sleeping tonight?"

"Absolutely," Havoc yawned into a stretch. Maynard thought it best to keep to himself how alluring he found the way Havoc's partially unbuttoned top and coat slipped off their elegant shoulder. Havoc caught Maynard ogling, fixed their coat, and smirked back at him. Maynard flushed, standing up to clear his throat before extending a hand to Havoc.

Havoc instead, clicked their teeth and swiped the carafe from Maynard's hand, addressing just a small fraction of their houseplant collection. The varied calathea survived the weeks without watering, but not unscathed; its variegated leaves drooped or curled into thin pipes. "Oh, that hospital is going to get an earful from me. Plants are completely innocent lifeforms; they don't deserve this!" He dumped the entire carafe over the planter. Maynard smacked his dry lips. Perhaps it was best not to drink so much before bed anyhow.

Even beyond the lab, their bedroom was Maynard's sanctuary from overstimulation. He filled his room, like the rest of the ship, with mid-century furniture he had collected in his youth, and it remained largely unchanged. When Havoc moved in, the couple's tastes blended seamlessly. Milky glass lamps lit the metal steps to their bed. Maynard dimmed the lights, transforming the dusk-like glow of the room's powder and periwinkle accents to one like twilight.

He took Havoc's hand and guided them up the steps to undress. When he was down to just a long-sleeve T-shirt and dress pants, he felt like holes were being stared into his back. "I'm so ready for bed, I can't believe it," he sighed.

Silence. He looked around for Havoc, but they were nowhere to be seen. His shoulders tensed.

"Boo!" Havoc's original form suddenly appeared, launching themself at Maynard like a jack-in-the-box.

"Lord!" Maynard fell backward onto the bed as Havoc snickered. This was one of their favorite tricks, and he fell for it every time. "Don't you think I've had enough pranks today?"

"You have a point." Havoc's gaze lowered. Maynard followed the stare; the fall had lifted his shirt. Havoc bit their lip, fixated on a sliver of abdomen peeking out. Although he was just ready for bed, the sudden simper was like water in Maynard's face. "Forgive me, starlight." Havoc shed their coat, letting it fall to the floor. "You just make it so easy."

They stalked along the bed in long strides. In slow, sensual motions they slipped off their high-heeled boots and unbuttoned the rest of their blouse. Maynard's stare fixated on their long legs, almost missing how, with the careful attention of a predator observing their prey, Havoc stared him down.

They crept over him. Fingertips slipped beneath the hem of his shirt. They purred into his ear, "I'm feeling rather inspired today, my star."

Maynard swallowed. "Is that so?" The words came out breathier than he intended. He wrapped his arms around his partner's lithe waist.

Their lips met. Quicker than he expected, the tender kiss deepened. Maynard wished to draw out the kiss, but he was more than happy to give Havoc what they demanded. His mouth pressed firmly against theirs, imploring Havoc to part their lips. They accepted his tongue with a sly giggle. Havoc transformed their throat, and a velvety suction latched onto Maynard's tongue. Maynard groaned, savoring the gentle massage, but he couldn't manage the kiss for long as the suction drew air from his lungs.

During a pause for breath, he gasped, "That feels amazing...." He grabbed Havoc's jaw and pried their mouth open to look inside. "Where does the air go?"

Havoc rolled their eyes. They grabbed his hand and slid their tongue up his index. The intense suction of his fingers in their mouth stopped his mind. "I would appreciate you shutting up now."

"Yes, dear."

Havoc kissed along the side of Maynard's neck, down his sternum, just off the straight surgical scar which reached almost to his stomach. The suction was sure to leave a few bruises. Maynard would be ashamed in the morning. Right now, it felt incredible. Havoc lifted Maynard's shirt to kiss each of his white inked star tattoos lightly before sinking their teeth into his pec. A pained and pleased grunt escaped Maynard's lips, eliciting a snicker from Havoc. They continued on a path of wanton inhaling down Maynard's body until they reached the hardening bulge beneath his pants.

Maynard propped himself up on his elbows so he could better see how they slid down his pants and stroked him over the cloth of his underwear. They kissed and nuzzled his cock into the crooks of their sharp features.

It took no time for Maynard to become erect. He was so stiff that when they pulled his boxers down, the tip of his dick caught on the waistband and sprang back up with a rebound. Havoc's titter at the awkward movement forced Maynard to throw his hands over his face as he sank into the bed.

"You are so lovely, my star." Some wonderful slipperiness wrapped around Maynard's cock. He came out of hiding to see Havoc had shifted their hand into something viscous and squishy—a favorite of Maynard's. "The way you glow excites me," Havoc growled. Maynard's breaths became long, matching the pace of Havoc's stroke. They looked up at him, ensuring solid eye contact again as they asked, "Are you enjoying this?"

"Yes."

"Yes?"

"Yes, my prince."

His politeness earned him a reward; Havoc slid their tongue along the shaft of his cock. With soft and slow laps, they made their way from the base of his shaft to wrap around the tip in torturous circles. His cock throbbed as they took it into their mouth, shallow at first. They cupped his testicles and their throat shifted again for more powerful suction. In sheer ecstasy, Maynard threw his head back, reveling in the perfect combination of Havoc's soft mouth and rough suck.

No matter how badly he wanted to, he was careful not to buck into their mouth. They opened their throat for him naturally. He gripped the sheets, so close to coming when they stopped. The second they surrendered him, all of Maynard's shyness faded. With terrible impatience, he pulled Havoc off their knees and threw them onto the bed. He crawled over Havoc in pursuit of the suctioned kisses, desperate for them. Havoc obliged.

Maynard tossed aside Havoc's belt and pants. He massaged their bottom and kissed their neck in a hurried attempt to relax them. The couple agreed on this; Havoc would never use their power to ease themself into penetration. Both of them found knowing Havoc's desire was genuine to be far more pleasurable, and Maynard adored the way they melted into his hands.

"Well, aren't you eager?" they teased breathlessly.

"Very." Maynard felt their hardness against him and knew he couldn't wait a moment longer. He grabbed the lube from their bedside table. "Havoc, can I...?" He trailed off, modesty returning.

Havoc's face broke into a devilish grin, teasing, "Use your words, starlight."

Maynard contemplated his word choice. He wanted to be a gentleman. "I...want to be...close."

"Hm. Vague," Havoc said, affecting an air of insouciance as they ran a single nail down his chest.

Maynard closed his eyes. The provocation was driving him to the brink. He steadied his breathing, trying to quell the lascivious appetite overtaking his ability to think straight. When he opened his eyes, he found the quelling much more challenging. Havoc's luxurious strands sprawled over their pillows. Their delicate pearly lips partly open in a breathtaking simper that struck him. Shapeshifting was unnecessary when Havoc was already so perfect.

But Maynard wasn't complaining.

"Your Highness," he pleaded, maintaining solid eye contact as he pushed past his shame. Havoc's eyes lit up. They craved to be venerated and their fierce expression of unbridled desire encouraged Maynard to continue. "May I please put my cock inside you?"

Havoc exhaled, undeniably aroused by the request. Lips grazed Maynard's earlobe as they whispered, "I would love that."

Maynard wasted no time. He popped the cap off the lubricant. With a slicked middle finger, he massaged their anus. Havoc's composure faded. They stifled their moans as he tended to the muscle.

Maynard fought to slow himself. He gave the massage a generous amount of time, relishing the gentle sighs, before he asked, "Are you ready?"

"Yes."

Maynard positioned himself on top of his partner and gently entered them. Enveloped in tension and warmth, he groaned. Havoc laced their fingers into his hair, clutching the back of his scalp. They gasped in his ear with each push.

Maynard listened intently to his beloved partner's moans; he knew where they wanted him. He gradually allowed himself to get lost in the gratification of Havoc's hole, warm and wet only for him. Only he got to see this darling, desperate side of Havoc.

They knew how to make him squirm as well. Havoc's claws extended, prodding into Maynard's shoulder as he picked up the pace. Maynard groaned their name as he rejoiced in the mixture of pain and pleasure. Havoc gratefully cried Maynard's name back to him. The sound gave Maynard goosebumps. Soon he lost total control of himself, shaking as he slipped in and out of their silky hole. He couldn't pull himself away even if he tried.

Shame abandoned him. He cried, cursed, and screwed his eyes shut as he came deep inside Havoc. They came shortly after, their limbs coiled tightly around him. With their concentration broken, the distraction caused all of their tricks to disappear. Maynard lay on top of them with no consideration for the stickiness. He desired only to be close.

"Sleep now, starlight." Havoc wrapped their arms around him.

"No, I should...." He panted for some time. "...help clean you up."

"I wasn't asking." Havoc slipped out from beneath Maynard, so he lay flat on his stomach. His muscles, as if stuffed with down, showed no defiance. Havoc removed Maynard's glasses and set them on the nightstand. Maynard only now realized he'd forgotten to take them off; it was a surprise they hadn't fallen. They stroked slow circles onto his chest. Maynard slowly drifted away, wondering how little sleep he had gotten in the last few days. Weeks, apparently. "Go to sleep," Havoc hummed. "The sooner you do, the sooner I'll get up."

With that agreement, Maynard faded into sleep.

Maynard kept his finger hovering over the volume button, ready to lower it at Havoc's slightest movement. A sense of duty jolted him awake after several hours of sound sleep, and with Havoc asleep for a change, a rare quiet moment presented itself—ideal for reviewing the station's security tape. He peeked from the screen every so often to admire the gentle tide of his partner's body as they breathed.

The station's lone camera resided just outside the supply room, and so much of the footage was unremarkable.

The silver lining being that–if Maynard absolutely had to find fault with his precious scanner–it didn't work as quickly or accurately as Havoc could. Anytime someone spoke, five minutes of footage became twenty minutes of translating voices over the grainy feed.

Only researchers en route to their workplace or sleeping chamber passed the frame. Naturally, they only entered the supply room when they needed something from inside it. Otherwise, it was mostly silent. From the other room, Maynard could often hear Dr. F'vr cursing or berating other researchers, often arrogant enough to belittle their scientific expertise. He based many of his rants on conspiracy theories or nonsensical hunches by other people who had no business giving medical advice. Dr. F'vr seemed to be no legitimate doctor; as far as Maynard could tell, the man did nothing more than bark orders. Maynard felt a sense of karmic justice in remembering the doctor's lifeless corpse.

Xijax's self-portrait was a striking likeness, showcasing grayish skin common amongst Qin, natives of Alqen. If Maynard recalled correctly, Xijax moved from Alqen, and used to work in delivery security. He could only assume the procedures diminished a broad frame more conventional to Qin.

The researchers tugged Xijax back and forth between rooms. His discomfort was apparent, but he rarely voiced it. At one point, he entered the operating room and never came out.

Nothing happened for some time. Through sped-up footage, Maynard watched a researcher roll the quantum tunneling device into the operating wing. They reappeared hours later and returned the machine to the supply room.

Maynard fast-forwarded through what he expected to be more days of nothing, but in a flash, complete pandemonium erupted. He reversed the footage. The camera shook, the picture distorted, and somewhere in the chaos, the creature boarded. Maynard was thankful for the moments of static censoring the violence as the creature shredded the researchers into pieces. Dr. F'vr sealed the operating room with the creature and other researchers inside and ran toward the cockpit. A few minutes later, the screen went to static. *The asteroid.*

Maynard combed through his beard in deep thought when he felt shuffling beside him. Havoc turned over to face Maynard and cuddled into his side drowsily. "Can't sleep, starlight?"

Maynard shone the screen toward his chest and away from Havoc's squint. He had no clue what time it was. "I'm sorry for disturbing you, darling."

"Make it up to me," Havoc mumbled lazily. "Get me a snail."

Maynard sucked in his cheek and weighed the consequences of the deal. "...To eat or as a pet?"

"Surprise me."

"Okay then." Maynard adjusted his glasses. "In exchange, I need one more thing."

"Forgiveness is a pretty big thing to ask for already. Father Luque will tell you that," Havoc said. Maynard eyed them. "Okay, fine. I'll get up."

Trophy Husband

Chapter 11

Vince crashed right into Maynard. It wasn't his fault, though. He was entering the kitchen just as the other man was rushing out. Lochlan stumbled into both of them, and Maynard barely kept his coffee from spilling.

"Vincent!" He was probably amazed to see Vince out in the open. He and Havoc shared a look, and whatever it meant, Vince didn't care.

His two weeks of solo-snooping had him feeling braver today. Once he realized nothing was going to leap out and electrocute him, he poked around in Havoc and Maynard's room. *Gossip is a sin*, he told himself. But so is arson, probably, and if he allowed himself a moment of real thought, he might have set the ship ablaze.

He learned a lot about his new roommates. Mainly, that he may have jumped to a few conclusions. First, Maynard was *super* blind. Vince found this out from a spare set of glasses lying around, with the left lens as thick as a matchbook. He read through a few of Maynard's personal logs, and sure enough, he was legally blind in one eye. That might explain all the scowls and narrowed glances. Second, Havoc—*Prince* Havoc—used to be rich. Like, fuck-you rich. And he thought Vince was spoiled. *So that's it.* Vince figured Havoc's lunacy must have stemmed from being born bored.

Third, most importantly, Vince found *tons* of photos of the crew in Lochlan's family albums. Havoc and Maynard grew up alongside Lochlan's sister, brother-in-law, and nieces. He flipped through decades of Christmases, birthdays, and school graduations. They seemed happier than Vince had ever seen them. Vince had been so wrapped up in the whirlwind of romance, he only then realized he hadn't even met Lochlan's family.

Maybe Lochlan's true soulmates were his friends. Vince was just an eclipse, a dark spot on an otherwise brilliant system. Yes, his morbid curiosity got the better of him, and he ended up reading a few of the astronomy books lying around. Horrible idea. Now he knew about a thousand more ways he could die out here, but whatever.

For the love of his life, Vince decided he could grin and bear whatever torture the others had in store for him today. With one goal in mind, he set out this morning: he,

Maynard, and Havoc were going to learn to tolerate each other.

"Watch where you're going," Lochlan groused at Maynard. He moved Vince into the kitchen by the shoulders and headed straight for the coffeemaker.

"Sorry. Good morning."

Vince felt suspicious when Maynard suddenly turned around to follow them, but he wore a natural smile and chimed back, "Good morning, Maynard. How did you sleep?"

"He didn't." Havoc sat at the kitchen island, elbows on the table, reading. Beside him sat a cool glass of orange juice and tonic with a thick float of espresso. Rumors said Maynard and Havoc enjoyed fancy coffees, and Vince assumed this would be the only thing they ever found in common before he realized Havoc was reading *Candide*.

Vince could hit himself. *Duh. Everyone likes music.* To a Chorister, music was the language of the spirit. Perhaps the clergy emphasized 'superior' genres of music, but Vince never preached that. He thought everyone should listen to music they like and find value in it. This didn't make him popular among the priesthood, but everyone he counseled found it easier to talk to him when they realized he kept an open mind. Vince wondered if Havoc might enjoy the operetta as much as he was clearly enjoying the book with its many dog-eared corners and annotations.

"Coulda guessed that." Lochlan pointed at Maynard's eyebags.

Maynard peered into the back of a spoon; dark, thin skin circled his bottom lashes. "Yes. I was up late…working something out."

Lochlan took a seat at the island next to them. "Let me guess. Hawk?"

Havoc stirred their drink, eyes still glued to their book. "You know it." Vince snorted. He probably wasn't supposed to hear that. Maynard's cheeks reddened. He cleared his throat, a subtle plea to change the subject.

It was clear he wanted to discuss something work-related. Vince took the hint and headed for their pantry—which he'd spent the better part of a day re-organizing—and pulled together some items for breakfast along with a baggie of cinnamon sticks, cloves, and a small cone of piloncillo. Lochlan teased him for smuggling it onboard like contraband, but without this precious parcel of coffee add-ins to remind him of home, he definitely would have lost his shit. He tossed everything into a pot with some water and waited for the water to boil as Lochlan and his friends continued tormenting each other.

Maynard, tired of being talked over, finally blurted out, "Havoc called the hospital." The sudden shift in mood made Vince want to take a peek at the crew.

Lochlan's frown lines creased. "Can't I get something to eat before we get into all this?"

Havoc picked up the cue to speak, sighing, and closing their book. "The hospital reports no missing stations. In fact, they don't even have the funding for stations. And they are familiar with exactly zero of the doctors named in Xijax's journal." They held up a hand in the shape of a zero.

"I sent you the security footage, but it wasn't much help either."

"So we've got no leads," Lochlan said.

"Well, we have one lead...." Maynard leaned in to whisper. He peeked over his shoulder, and Vince's eyes darted away.

Vince kind of wished he could do something to help. He couldn't help but feel frustrated too. Despite his worries about them returning to the station, he found himself invested in the mission now as a victim of its weirdness. At the very least, there was nothing a cup of coffee couldn't fix, so he got to work on a café de olla for his husband.

Lochlan slapped the counter. "Ha! Yeah, I don't think he's gonna be all that willing to talk to us."

"Right. Not us, but...." Maynard whispered again.

"No. No! Are you fucking crazy?"

Vince tucked a cinnamon stick into a mug and turned around to check out the commotion. All eyes were on him. "Uh." Their eyes followed him as he set the mug down in front of Lochlan. "Is there something on my face?"

Lochlan's rigid expression suddenly brightened. "Nope. Thank you, sweetheart."

"Convincing." Vince now understood that whenever his husband brushed something aside, it was probably a big deal. "Seriously, what?"

Lochlan stuck his tongue into his cheek before answering, "Alright, you got me. Do you think I should dye my hair? You know, make me look younger."

Vince threw a hand over his mouth, offended even to hear the worst idea in the history of man. Right after murder and shell suits. "What? No! Absolutely not! You are not touching a hair on that gorgeous head." Vince combed through Lochlan's soft, perfectly silver strands with his fingers.

Lochlan took Vince's hand and kissed it. "Thanks, sugar." He looked up at Maynard past his brow. "See, Pierce? Let's just leave it alone."

It was just weird. All day Vince felt like holes were being burrowed into him. That it was *ten* fucking degrees in here could have been a factor, but unease followed him everywhere.

Lochlan didn't help. It was like every time someone else walked into the room, he couldn't leave fast enough. Not to mention Maynard and Havoc's energies were just off. Specializing in necromancy made Vince sensitive to all life forces and—while the emotional energy hadn't been stellar before—the vibe between the friends was especially hostile today. Lochlan kept asking Vince to head back to their bedroom. Vince wanted to believe Lochlan was simply sparing him from bullying, but he felt he'd made it clear enough that he was no longer an easy target and he was not letting this burst of determination go to waste. He skimmed off the nerves and continued floating from room to room like he actually lived there.

After confirming the trophy room was empty, Lochlan loosened up. Returning to his playful self, he even offered Vince an 'exclusive,' 'behind-the-scenes' tour of the room.

The trophy room, and its many glass cases, housed the treasures of the crew's adventures. Copies of rare books, replicas of artifacts, and gifts from those they helped packed the room. Lochlan exuded confidence, guiding them through the room with a warm, nostalgic humor and a hand on the small of Vince's back. Vince melted when Lochlan showed him a rusted plastic button pin of a flower from a little girl whose parents they rescued from a Venusian landslide.

Call him cliché, but Vince found the heroism undeniably sexy. He could not keep his hands off of Lochlan, and they ended up stopping between every story just to make out.

"I'll be right back." Lochlan kissed Vince on the cheek and headed for the restroom.

"Don't be long," Vince sang.

He ran a finger along the edge of the case housing a broken pair of wire-frame glasses. What kind of mysterious or glamorous past did this hold? These stories helped Vince picture how he could fit into Lochlan's life; cheering for him from the sidelines, welcoming him home after missions, and when he finally retired, finding a cozy home together.

Vince sighed at the dreamy vision when Maynard's face suddenly emerged from the opposite side of the glass. "Vincent."

"Oh my gods!" Vince almost knocked over the display. Using both hands, he steadied it and scowled. "Not to be rude but are you and Havoc *aware* that you shouldn't sneak up on people?"

"Yes!" Maynard whispered and stepped out from behind the pedestal. He acted like an intruder in his own house. "I do know that. I'm sorry, I'm a bit on edge." He stood a bit too close, repeatedly looking over Vince's shoulder.

Vince took a step back. "And maybe a little sleep-deprived?"

Maynard brought his fingertips to his eyebags. "Is it obvious?"

"...No." Of course it was.

For a second, Maynard got lost in the tender rub of his fingers against his dry eyes, and Vince tried to sneak away. Maynard snapped back into the moment. "May I speak with you?"

"Uhm...." Vince looked around. No Lochlan. Everything in him told him to leave, but he forced an awkward smile and said, "Sure."

"I'm curious about the limits of your magical abilities."

"Oh!" Vince's posture naturally straightened. How could he forget? Maynard wanted to chat about that spell. The question stirred up a passion in Vince that had been asleep for years. Leaving the church gave him little opportunity to practice, but magic remained an integral part of his life. Unfortunately, when other people found out he was a spellcaster, they always asked him the dumbest questions. "Do you, like, saw people in half?" or "How many wishes do I get?" Even worse, they usually asked him to perform so he'd make a cup move or light a candle. That was already more than most could handle. Nobody appreciated the good stuff. Not in the way Maynard seemed to. "Okay, I'm happy to share."

Maynard's eyes lit up as he pulled out a small notepad. "You're able to commune with the dead. Is that right?"

"That's right. As long as they want to commune with me. I'm open."

"So, if you came across a body, do you believe you could—"

"Vinni!" Lochlan bellowed, charging back into the room. "That coat you texted me? I just saw it."

Vince immediately abandoned the discussion. That quilted leather and the way its drool-worthy emerald hue would flatter his complexion were way more important. "What did you think?"

Lochlan lowered his lids and guided Vince out of the room. "I think you'd look pretty good in it. Let's pick it up today."

"Really?" A break from the ship? Vince could just cry. He completely forgot about Maynard and hurried for the exit. "Thank you, Loch. I have been feeling so cooped up. Wait." He stopped and pointed at Lochlan's arm. "Can you drive like this?"

"No. He can't," Maynard said.

Lochlan licked his teeth. "Good point. I'll teach you how to drive a shuttle." Vince had to learn eventually, but a trip all the way to the nearest planet on his first try sounded like a funeral waiting to happen. He gave Lochlan a terrified grimace. "Okay, fair. Hey, you ever seen Lord of the Rings? I've got a drinking game we can play. Come on."

Vince was tugged by his wrist. "Right now?" That beautiful, stupidly expensive coat was slipping away from him.

"If you want to finish by dinner tomorrow, we gotta get started."

Vince couldn't bring himself to ruin Lochlan's eager expression. He hadn't seen the movies, and a drinking game did sound fun. "That's cute. I totally didn't peg you as a Tolkien guy."

"Oh, I'm full of surprises."

"Lochlan!" Maynard shouted. "You can't keep dodging this!"

Vince moved back, inspecting the other men with narrowed eyes. They refused to meet his gaze. "Dodging what?"

Lochlan pointed a stern finger at Maynard. "Don't answer that."

Maynard removed his glasses to rub his eyes. "We've hit a dead end on the mission, and I think you can help." Lochlan threw his arm into the air.

"Me?" Vince asked. Unless they were hard-pressed for snacks, he could do nothing for them.

Lochlan placed a hand on Vince's shoulder. "Vinni, ignore him. He needs a nap. We're leaving."

Vince pulled back. "What's going on?"

"Aw, what's wrong, Laney?" Havoc's voice came from nowhere. Lochlan stepped aside to reveal they were standing right behind him. "Don't want your hubby tagging along? Cramping your style?"

"Where the hell did you come from?"

"I've been here the whole time."

"*Hello?*" The old men were too much for Vince today. "What are we talking about?"

Maynard stepped forward. "I want to see if you can communicate with the corpse we found."

Vince's ears twitched. How convenient that Lochlan left out the part about finding a dead body. *Wait.* Oh Gods. Maynard and Havoc were being serious. They actually wanted Vince's help.

A window in the depths of Vince's spirit creaked open, and in the fresh breeze, the service bell had rung for him once again. To his surprise, its call still drew him. He'd once left that call behind for the prospect of a real life, but maybe, just this one time, Vince could have it all. It could be a sign. The first in a long time.

"No." Lochlan looked Maynard in the eyes as he spoke to Vince. "You're not doing that."

Vince knocked Lochlan's hand off his shoulder. "Excuse you. I can speak for myself."

Lochlan's head and voice sank. "Vinni...." He seemed genuinely sorry, but he should know better. Being ordered around like that reminded Vince of all the parts he hated about the priesthood.

"Vincent, Lochlan is just worried about you." Even if he meant well, Maynard's attempt to manage the situation only made Vince feel more disregarded.

"He doesn't think you can handle it," Havoc sneered. "Now personally, *I'd* feel insulted, but, as we established, you can speak for yourself."

Lochlan's outstretched arm severed the group. "Everybody stop. This conversation is over."

"And what if I say it isn't?" Vince felt like he had aged backward. Heat pooled in his fingertips.

Lochlan's brow settled firmly over his eyes and his jaw clenched. Vince had seen this cross face before, but never pointed in his direction. "I don't want you to get hurt. It's not all fun and games down there. It can get...." His nostrils flared with a deep exhale like he was trying to calm himself down. "...intense. You're not an 'intense' kind of guy."

Vince crossed his arms. "What does that mean?"

"Nothing bad! No one thinks that's a bad thing! Right?" Lochlan looked to his companions for a lifeline. Havoc pursed their lips and said nothing.

"Right. Of course." Maynard nodded.

"I mean, we spent the day fighting a monster, and you got to hang out. Chill by the pool, watch movies. That's not a bad setup, right?"

Vince scoffed. Apparently, Lochlan's friends weren't alone in thinking Vince was just there to mooch. Maynard and Havoc took a sharp inhale and a step back. Socially clumsy as they were, it seemed even they could tell this wasn't heading in the right direction.

Vince folded his arms. "I like to unwind. Fine. But I am all alone up here. When I'm not bored, it's terrifying."

"It's terrifying *down there*." Lochlan placed a hand on Vince's cheek. His angry expression softened in such a way that it almost made Vince feel bad for getting so fired up. "Vinni...this isn't the cathedral."

A sizzling sound came from Vince, and Lochlan reeled back, fanning his fingers like he had touched a hot stove. "I need a minute, but, for the record, this conversation is not over." A dark aurora clouded Vince's sight as he left. His mind was everywhere, but he hung behind the door for a moment to eavesdrop.

"I really think this could be the key to everything." Maynard knew his best friend's stubbornness better than anyone.

But he had to know how stubborn Havoc was too. "Tell me, Lochlan. Which of these cases did you have in mind for Vince? I think he'd prefer a pedestal by the window."

"Okay, that's it!"

There were sounds of struggle before Maynard yelled, "Stop! You are such children! Havoc. Out. Now." When Vince heard Havoc's heel approaching, he ducked into the war room next door. Havoc stormed off muttering under their breath. After a stiff silence, Maynard added, "I've crossed a line too. I'm sorry."

"Whatever," Lochlan groaned. "I don't have time for you right now. I've got bigger problems."

Whether you're circling the Track or fortune hunting in the casino, one thing you can always bet on is seeing someone enjoy the smooth and savory taste of Diamond Cut Cigarettes. All-natural "ingredients" imported straight from Earth. Low in nicotine, high in quality.

DIAMOND CUT CIGARETTES

Warning: The Surgeon General has determined that cigarette smoking is dangerous to your health. But what do they know? What are they? Some kinda doctor? They can't tell me what to do. I'd like to see them try! Oh, what are you gonna do, Mx. Surgeon Ge-ne-ral? Deploy your army of surgeons on me? What, are they gonna suture me to death? Cut me open and harvest my organs? Actually, that sounds kind of scary. Uh, nevermind. If you're the surgeon general, this was all a joke. This is Randy from Accounting, by the way. NOT Patricia from Marketing. She's a good person who deserves to keep all her organs. Not like me, I'm a jerk who takes her yogurt out of the fridge, and I talk too much about my high school glory days. You're a grown man, Randy! Move on! Anyway, buy more cigarettes. But not more than the surgeon general would recommend!

Gross. Gross. Gross.

Chapter 12

//Havoc

Havoc gave themself a pat on the back for the clever bit. Shifted into a literal fly on the wall, they stalked the bickering newlyweds up and down the hall.

Lochlan chased after Vince. "Okay, so you're bored. Let's get you in a club or a job or something. Hey, you could deliver the mail!" He received the side-eye. "Not a mailman. Got it. Space flight attendant! You would make a *very cute* flight attendant." Lochlan grabbed Vince's waist flirtatiously and spun him around. He truly was the king of idiots.

Vince pushed away. "I'm going to ignore how correct you are and remind you I am already a very cute *spellcaster*! Definitely the cutest priest at the Cathedral Basilica of the Radiant Choir."

Lochlan apparently did not consider that a big deal. He let go of Vince and turned to walk away, but now Vince followed. They had been doing this back-and-forth for about fifteen minutes now, and it was making Havoc dizzy. "Will you drop this? I'm not changing my mind!"

"It's something else, isn't it? Why can't I come along?"

Lochlan slapped his hand on his cheek and dragged it along the side of his face. "Mercy, *why* did I bring you on the ship?"

Vince stopped dead in his tracks; the ground singed beneath his heel. "Are you asking why you married me?"

"What? No! Don't do that! You know that's not what I mean!"

With a fiery flourish, Vince waved his hand in a square. Magical energy traced the perimeter of the hallway, and a wall conjured between the couple. "Don't follow me." Vince marched in the opposite direction, leaving his husband behind.

"Vince?" Lochlan slammed on the wall. "Vince, get back here!"

Havoc tracked the runaway groom to the elevator, headed for the Keel. Lochlan's sleeker luxury shuttles remained tucked away, but the crew's chunky Prometheus was still sitting out. After hopping into the shuttle, Vince struggled with the controls for a degrading amount of time before giving up and resting his head on the yoke.

Havoc shifted back into their original form beside him. "What are you doing?"

Vince jolted. "Oh my gods! Will you stop doing that?!" He pounded the dashboard. A near face-strike from an ember caused Havoc to jump. Vince brought a hand to cover his mouth with big repentant eyes as he said, "Oh! I'm so sorry, Havoc. I'm just trying to take the shuttle to literally anywhere but this stupid ship."

Havoc didn't want to state the obvious, but, "You don't know how to fly."

"I am not useless! I can figure it out!" Vince smashed random buttons. Fortunately for him, he had not actually turned on the shuttle; the Prometheus' destruction would guarantee a divorce.

Havoc tapped their foot. It was probably best not to engage, but where was the fun in that? Their new room-mate was long overdue for an interview anyhow. "Well, I'm heading to the nexus, so I need the shuttle. Can you have this mental collapse in your room?"

"There's a nexus near here?" Vince sat straight up. "Take me with you!" A faux thoughtful Havoc tapped their chin, and Vince brought his hands together in mock prayer. "I will stay out of your way, I promise. I just need some fresh air."

Havoc made a show of their 'disinterest,' waving a hand to shoo Vince to the passenger seat. "Fine, fine. Since I'm on my way anyhow."

It was a long and dull ride to The Point, the nearest nexus to Sterillis III. All the way, Vince remained silent, holding up his end of the deal even as Havoc swerved and hit the brakes. All they got out of him were crackling sparks as they took a nosedive into the entry terminal. *Not good enough.*

Nexuses existed off-orbit, floating in space like pit stops between planets. Some were simple spots for fueling up and grabbing a quick bite of food, while others acted much like plazas with full-sized shops, restaurants, and hotels. Havoc scanned the Point for anything resembling a bar. The moment they spotted a suitable row of businesses, they parked in a public hangar. As they exited the vehicle, Vince opened his mouth to say something but kept it to himself. Probably for the best. To argue with Havoc about the ludicrous concept of 'illegal' parking was a waste of time.

Havoc found it challenging to guess the type of bar a priest might patron and landed on Club Sanity. Through the thick of tobacco and cannabis from the crowd outside, Roman columns and projected pole dancers decked the outside. Vince appeared pleased with the stylish interior, snapping a photograph of himself beside the illuminated, wavy, neon green bar top and its animal print velvet stools.

He turned to walk away but, before he could object, Havoc grabbed his elbow and headed for the bar. "I'm actually glad you begged to come along." They took a seat and patted the stool next to them. "I'm not allowed to use the credit card, so you spared me the effort of stealing it."

Vince sat down. "Okay...." He fumbled with his comm against the reader until it registered Lochlan's account successfully. "Now what?"

"Order?" Havoc waved to a group of attractive bartenders.

Vince resembled a dog with its tongue lolling out. "The bartenders are hot."

The Father's vulgar remark took Havoc by surprise. They studied Vince's expression, and under their gaze, he appeared to shrink.

A Martian bartender walked over; the small antennas sprouting from his crown bobbed as he approached. His green skin and blue hair gleamed in the neon light. He leaned over the counter with a flirtatious grin. "Gentlemen, how lovely to see you this evening. What can I get you?"

Vince thought. "Stupid question, do you have tequila?"

Havoc snorted. "Why not? I'll have the same." The bartender stepped away to prepare their drinks, leaving the two to sit in uncomfortable silence. "You can relax. Most businesses in the Milky Way carry popular Earth products. Think of it like...imports from another country."

"So I'm guessing the further out you get, the harder things are to find?"

"If I were you, I wouldn't present that bill to your husband."

Out of the corner of his eye, Havoc observed Vince pull his old cell phone from his back pocket and tap away at the screen. He opened U-link, a popular social media app among young people throughout the galaxies. Vince's brow turned up at the sight of his own posting, a picture of his face buried in Lochlan's cheek. He locked the screen and stared blankly at the wall of bottles across from him.

The bartender dropped off their drinks in chubby fluted glasses with a wedge of lime. Vince snickered to himself at the off choice of glassware but didn't bother to correct them. At least the lime looked marvelous and juicy in the light. Havoc popped the fruit into their mouth and held up their glass to Vince. "*Salud.*"

Vince's eyebrows raised. He seemed more surprised by the cheers than by the choice of snack. "*Salud.*"

From over the rim of his cup, Havoc watched Vince take a modest sip, then silently return the glass to the table. While most should be cautious around Havoc, Vince seemed especially reserved. The man Lochlan gushed over, the man who pranked Havoc yesterday; this was not the same man. The impulse to upset a drink or shake Vince just to get a reaction was unbearable.

Vince peeked at Havoc. "Need something?" They asked.

"No. Just looking around." Vince glanced back at his phone.

Another slow sip. They were on track to achieve nothing. Havoc trilled their fingers on the table, plotting before saying, "I agree with you. The bartender is insanely hot."

Vince gave a slight, skeptical smile. "Right?"

"And he was definitely flirting with us."

"Ha, I—" Vince checked himself with a hem. "Didn't notice." He opened his phone again.

Havoc grated their teeth. It was time to send in the headliners. "So. Lochlan says that you know some interesting drinking games."

Vince sat up like a puppy expecting a treat. "I know a few, yeah! ...Do you want to play something?"

He really was too easy. "Hmmm. I *was* looking forward to a nice and quiet outing, but sure."

From the inside pocket of his long fur-trimmed coat, Vince revealed a black, leather pouch with a calligraphic 'V' embroidered on the back and a silver clasp shaped like a flower fastening the front. Vince stiffened up when he noticed Havoc's astonishment. "Did Lochlan warn you I can go kinda overboard?"

Havoc threw their head back into a cackle. "*Please.* I think I can keep up with a choirboy!"

Vince licked his teeth. "Okay." With a smug smirk, he offered Havoc a straw plucked from the bar tray, taking one for himself. "Show me what you've got, Your Highness."

Only someone with a death wish should drink this much. Vince's constitution floored Havoc. From classy sipping to straw sucking and shots, the night escalated with a certain Lochlan quality about it. Vince was bold enough to hit on the bartender, persuading him to leave the bottle.

Unfortunately, the good-natured soul's assumption that Havoc would play a fair game was a regrettable one. In due time, Vince was drunk enough to spill his guts, all while Havoc teetered on the line at tipsy.

"Am I an idiot?" With a clumsy toss, Vince sent bone dice onto the counter, where they nearly tumbled off. "Should I not even be here?"

"Poor thing...perhaps not." Havoc rolled a two and a four, defeating Vince's two and three. "Drink up," they taunted. They shapeshifted their hand back to standard, non-sticky skin before their opponent could notice.

Vince took a penalty sip of his drink. "Oh no...." He brought his forehead to the bar top. "I'm never going to get that apartment back," he garbled.

"I wonder who'll get the kids in the divorce?"

"No roommates...Lower East Side...five-minute walk to the station." Vince lamented this to the counter.

"Maynard should stay with Lochlan. Which means I'm stuck with you."

"It was a *really* nice apartment."

Havoc snorted. "Lochlan made it sound like a shit-hole."

"Of course he fucking did!" Vince slapped the counter. "Asshole!"

"Hear, hear!"

Vince chuckled. Rubbing his eyes, he sighed, "I said I was going to stay out of your way...."

Havoc shrugged. "I'm enjoying the show. Although it's not helping me understand what you see in the old lubber."

Vince looked up, ice-cold, as he delivered, "I'm here for his money." Havoc choked; their drink sputtered out. Vince howled a laugh at their expense, and Havoc laughed too. The glee tapered into a nostalgic exhale. "I don't even know where to start," Vince said. "I didn't know I liked him right away. I mean, I thought he was hot. Like, objectively, but he was such a dick the first time I met him."

"Tell me about it. Lochlan was shy with the details. According to him, a 'spy' walked up to the door." Havoc smiled at the memory of Lochlan blushing red to his ears, asserting, "no way in hell that guy is a mailman" and that he now understood every joke that had the punchline of mailmen siring bastard children.

"So, the base was on my delivery route, right?" Vince started. "It was my first day, and I was super behind. I was already tired, and this scary guy outside his scary house started yelling at me, so I kinda blew up at him. I thought he was gonna get me fired, but then he came up to me all shy and started cracking jokes. Every time I stopped by, he 'just so happened' to be outside." Vince's stare softened, melting like agave in his glass. "He'd ask me about my day and make me laugh. It was just a silly little crush I had. I didn't take it seriously because I didn't think he would either. It's so hard to make friends when you're an adult." Havoc was painfully aware of that. "I dated around. A lot, actually." On recalling his days on the market, Vince clutched his drink in one hand and his head in the other. "Bringing him his mail became my favorite part of the day, and...one day I thought about the people in his life, and I thought, 'Gods, I just want someone to love me that much.' Then I realized I wanted *Lochlan* to love me that much." Vince took a sip of his drink to hide his perfectly pink expression. "I had this full-blown, head-over-heels, totally self-esteem destroying type of crush on him. I was way too chicken to do anything about it. When he asked me out, I couldn't believe it. But now we're married, I'm on this Godsforsaken ship with you three...and I've never been happier."

"I see." Lost in Vince's tender words about Lochlan, a sickeningly sweet feeling blossomed in Havoc's chest. Noticing the light conjuring in Vince's glistening eyes, they questioned whether to retreat before some bizarre reaction sprang forth.

"And I know you probably don't want to hear this, but he is so good in bed."

A laugh burst from Havoc, jarred with the sudden mood shift. "At least he's good for something!"

"He really is my dream guy, which is why I'm...." Vince looked far away.

Havoc took another sip of their drink, goading, "Well, don't leave me guessing. You wouldn't want that."

"I shouldn't. He's your friend."

"Friend? What friend? I hardly know the man."

Vince's lips curled into a somber smile. "I'm freaking out. I just know he's it—he's the one—but what if he's thinking he made a mistake?" Havoc recalled Lochlan's similar words from the station. They attempted to slough off the unwelcome warm and fuzzies. Vince twirled his necklace with his fingers. He obviously wanted to ask Havoc what they knew, but stopped himself. "I probably seem pretty pathetic right now."

"Only very."

Vince sank onto the counter. "Ugh. Please don't tell anybody this. He probably told you I can be a little vain." He held up a pinched thumb and index finger.

"Pfft! No one has to tell anyone that. You're like a parakeet. I warned Lochlan to make sure that when you said 'yes' to his proposal that you hadn't just caught your own reflection."

Vince laughed into his palms. "Okay fair. I don't really try to hide it."

"Isn't vanity a sin, Father?" Havoc taunted, swallowing the last of their drink.

Vince recoiled, scrunching up his nose and sticking out his tongue. "Oh, bleh. Don't call me that!"

Havoc's brow arched. "It's your title, isn't it?"

"Not anymore." Vince swirled his drink.

Perhaps Havoc could finally diagnose the root of Vince's disastrous decision making. "I never understood abandoning all that power to become a mailman."

"It just wasn't right. I wasn't right. I was good at it, but it wasn't what I wanted."

"You stuck around."

"Of course I did. What else was I going to do? I was raised into the position. Can I tell you a secret?" Vince leaned in. "I snuck out all the time."

Havoc grinned. "*Really?*"

"I'd go into the city at night in a hoodie and sun-glasses. I looked like a burglar. It was so stupid," Vince laughed. "From the moment I could speak, this was it. But I actually...." Vince took a deep breath. He paused, looking around the bar as if unsure he wanted to say his next words out loud. "I actually didn't leave the church so much as I was *asked* to leave."

"Aren't you the chosen one or whatever they call it?"

"Conductor. But, yeah. This wild magic condition I have can be a little...much for other people. You might be surprised, but I'm actually doing better than I was. Which is crazy, because I did *everything* they told me to. I got up, I prayed, I did my chores, I prayed, I went to bed. They did their best to fill my day with tasks to keep my mind 'free from sin' but I can't help it. Sometimes I would start to worry. And when I worry, I can be a lot, and I am always worried. I was told that if I gave up my magic, I'd be 'healed' and I could live a normal life, but my God, Xovivos, chose *me*. And I want to believe that everything happens for a reason. Long story short, the church did this big, dumb ceremony to pray for a new champion. A better one. They didn't get one and none of us took that well. So they asked me to leave because I wasn't of any good use."

"I understand," Havoc related more than they were willing to admit. "You may find this shocking, but I wasn't known for my 'good will' back home."

"Well, now you help others. I don't do anything." Vince was quiet for a long time. "Havoc?"

"Yes?"

"Do you miss being a prince?"

Havoc thought for a moment. A fortune beyond measure and an entire planet at their beck and call? They missed that, sure. But bartering with their parents for the lives of families and friends over petty offenses? "No."

"I don't miss being a priest, but sometimes I miss being important."

Gods damn it. Havoc fought against the tightness in their chest to no avail. They never expected to find kinship in Lochlan's late-life crisis. Havoc too had once joined the crew for love, following Maynard on his grand quest to make the universe a better place, whatever the hell that meant. They found the work gave them fleeting feelings of redemption. Perhaps, with time, they could leave the universe a better place than they found it. A net positive. That's all they asked.

Havoc's reign on Tsytaas, their home planet, began and ended in unnecessary bloodshed. The former, a centuries-old quarrel of their ancestors, which led to their family's deplorable reign, and the latter their own when that reign finally ended. All they took from ruling was a well-deserved curse, banishment, and centuries of agony weighing on their soul. For many years, Havoc roamed a Sterillis planet in the Milky Way, dying and reincarnating.

Dying and reincarnating. Still, it was only a fraction of the cruelty they inflicted on others. Havoc found it ironic now to be seated next to someone who made death their business.

"Oh!" Vince's face lit up. "I love this song."

As a woeful pop tune filled the bar, Havoc chuckled. Vince performed into his cup a sloppy rendition of *Hopelessly Devoted to You* with imprecise lyrics. He was definitely drunk, but damn it if he didn't have the stage presence. With a blonde wig and a porch set, he'd be ready for the screen. "This is a weird song for this bar to play, right?" Vince said between verses.

Havoc smiled into their cup. "I requested it."

Vince continued swaying to the beat. "Why?"

"The visual of you having an emotional breakdown to this song made me think of the musical. I thought it would be entertaining."

"You're such a dick," Vince shoved them, giggling.

"At least if you stick around you can help me drag Lochlan to shows."

Vince narrowed his eyes, on the verge of something. All of a sudden, Havoc felt like a wild animal hidden in the bushes. "Havoc...why are you getting in the middle of this?"

"Because it's funny," they shrugged.

"No, really."

"Because it's really funny?"

"I don't think you mean that." Vince stared intensely, his gaze sharp as aimed arrows. Havoc's leg bounced as they searched the bar for a new topic.

"I think you're actually *trying* to be nice *and* I think you're doing this for Lochlan." Vince's eyes widened, like a hunter's searchlights. Frozen in place, Havoc feared the slightest movement would expose them. "Oh, I'm right, aren't I? You want things to be okay between me and him because...you *looove* him."

Havoc slammed onto the counter, combating the warmth rushing to their cheeks. "Ha! That is hilarious! You have officially had too much to drink."

"Oh, you two are so alike! All prickly on the outside, ooey-gooey on the inside." Vince leaned forward.

Havoc leaned back in their chair as far as possible. "Maybe it's time I got you home."

"And you don't even want the credit! You're such a good friend," Vince trilled, wiping away...an actual tear?

Havoc stood. "Okay! We're leaving before one of us throws up!"

"No!" Vince threw back another shot. "We're going dancing!"

Havoc shriveled. "What have I done?"

Vince hooked his arm into Havoc's. "Oh, you've done it alright! Bad news, babe, I'm ooey-gooey all over and I'm a great dancer!"

A smile broke across Havoc's face at Vince's spirited merengue. "Ugh. I can't bring you back like this anyway. The lubber will crush me to death."

Huff and Puff
Chapter 13

//Lochlan

The artificial sun forced Lochlan to squint. He turned the dial down on the bio-dialer and the bulbs lining the glass dome above him dimmed to an overcast.

The Stern was the closest thing the ship had to an outdoor space. Back in the days of constructing Leviathan's Luck, Maynard gave Lochlan free rein to design the area however he wanted. Lochlan took building the Stern more seriously than he had most things in his life. In his book, a place to unwind was just as necessary a safety feature as life rings. Between comfortable seating and rich foliage, sat yard games, a hot tub, and a respectable outdoor kitchen complete with grill and brick oven. Lochlan leaned back to take in the softer sunlight, remembering how it kept you from going crazy.

"There you are." Maynard stepped out from the glass double doors that led to the rest of the ship.

Lochlan changed the channel. He couldn't let Maynard catch him moping over Pretty Woman for the second time today. "Hey," he choked, wafting smoke away from him. It didn't help. Now he was just waving the cigarette in front of his face.

"I should have guessed I would find you out here." Maynard took a seat beside him in a matching wooden deck chair. "Are you okay?"

Lochlan rubbed his eye with his thumb. "Yeah. Down right peachy."

"Pretty Woman?"

"What is that, a movie? Never heard of it." Lochlan avoided looking at the projector. The savory scent of smoke floating on the breeze distracted Maynard. He stared at Lochlan's carton of cigarettes. He should be proud he held out so long before swiping one. A whole minute. "Hawk's gonna get mad at you."

Maynard pulled a brass lighter from his pocket. "Yes, well, right now, I'm mad at them too." Even if he wanted Maynard to stop for his heart's sake, Lochlan never gave his best friend grief about smoking. They picked it up together as teenagers, and quit so many times just to fold at the first signs of hassle. Their line of work included plenty of hassle.

"Whatever," Lochlan shrugged. "It's your funeral."

Maynard laid back in the seat and closed his eyes. "I should reconsider then. I've had enough of those for the week."

Lochlan snorted. "Yeah, that was a good one." The prank idea shocked Vince, but Lochlan had no doubts that Maynard would treat it like a day at the carnival.

"My untimely death? Glad you enjoyed yourself."

Lochlan whacked Maynard only to be whacked back. "Don't be like that. I saw your face."

"What are you talking about? It hurt like hell." Lochlan's smirk suggested he wasn't buying it. "Fine. It was...interesting." Maynard shifted in his seat but the look would not let up. "Exhilarating! You win! Now stop looking at me like that." He pulled up his log and raised his comm to show off eight pages of the juicy details. "I still need to ask Vincent about the specifics."

"Well, that'll cheer him up. He loves talking about that kinda stuff."

"Yeah," Maynard put his comm down and returned to his cigarette with a reflective draw. "I really thought he didn't like magic."

Lochlan wasn't sure if Maynard was serious. It was like wondering if Maynard 'liked' science. Spend five seconds with the dork and it should be pretty obvious. "Where did you get that?"

"You said he hardly uses it."

Lochlan's lips stretched. "It's not like it's a hiring requirement for the post office. Anyway, he says it spooks people."

"But you don't have a problem leaving out important details. You told me he left the church."

"Ah, he doesn't do so well with getting bossed around." Lochlan smirked. "Remind you of anyone?"

A sarcastic "You," came from both of them, followed by a joint laugh.

They gazed out at the dome together. It reminded Lochlan of being a kid, stargazing with Maynard on a chilly rooftop in Brooklyn. They could hardly make a thing out, but when they saw something, man did they get fired up.

Smoke billowed from Maynard's nostrils. "An issue with authority...." It was the same reason he left Echelon and Lochlan ditched the Earth altogether. Maynard's rebellious phase came late, but Lochlan's started the day he was born with still no end in sight, but Leviathan's Luck was about more than just working for themselves. Out in the universe, they were free from the endless red tape and wire-pulling that blocked them from actually helping other people. Some may call them crazy, but they believed a person was worth more than whatever a bunch of tight-asses wrote on a piece of paper. It meant everything to Lochlan that Vince shared the same attitude.

Lochlan wanted a distraction from today, but after a long sobering silence, he caved. "Be honest with me. Am I being an asshole?"

"Yes. But so are we." Maynard tucked his hands behind his head.

"All I want is to keep Vinni away from that thing. Can't we just bring the body here?"

Maynard pushed his tongue around his teeth. "We're not sure what the source of the time anomaly is, how it works, or the extent of its power. All we know is that it's not affecting us right now. I suspect that is because the ship is out of its range. It would be more dangerous to bring anything from the station on board."

"You let Hawk bring snacks."

"I threw those away at the station."

Lochlan huffed. "Well, what'd you do that for? The source isn't gonna be ice cream."

"Save it. I've heard it already." Maynard kept his eyes closed, resting in the palm of his hand. "Lochlan, come on, man. You know I wouldn't ask if it weren't important."

"Yes, you would," Lochlan said. As much as Maynard would like to sell himself as this wise and all-knowing sage of a man, he did a lot of dumb shit just to see what would happen. Maybe he wanted to test Vince. See how committed he really was.

"I'm less careful when it's just us. Fine. But you really think I'd put someone else in danger for no reason? Why?

To see some magic? Chase him away? Listen, however I feel about your relationship doesn't matter right now. Vincent is a professional. He's right here, and he can help. He wants to."

Lochlan fidgeted with the filter end of his cigarette, flicking embers into the air. No matter what anyone said, he couldn't be convinced that this would be anything like what Vince had dealt with in the past. "That thing shredded my arm like it was nothing. You know how tough that is. I'm supposed to sit back and act like it can't hurt him, too?"

Maynard leaned over to place a hand on Lochlan's chair. "As long as it remains behind that door, nothing can happen to him. It's an unnerving environment, I'll give you that, but all he needs to do is come down and see if Dr. F'vr wants to talk." He had that look in his eye; fierce determination and total fixation that said he'd die on this hill. It wasn't easy to impress Dr. Maynard 'uhm, actually' Percival. He was the guy who thought he could do everybody's job better than they could. Asking for Vince's help showed high praise. Lochlan hated how well he knew that. Maynard swung his legs back over the side of the chair and tapped his cigarette against the ashtray. "I should have talked to you first."

"No," Lochlan sighed, sitting up too. "You were right to drop it on him. I never would have let him know."

Maynard's brows lifted. "What are you saying?"

"Nothing online, nothing on the station...." Lochlan put his cigarette out. "I hate to say it, but it's not like I've got any better ideas."

Maynard had trouble keeping a straight face. He looked afraid to make any sudden movements just in case it might scare Lochlan off. It really could have. "Well, I have been trying to come up with something else."

"You're no good at keeping the peace. Just quit while you're ahead."

Maynard rubbed his palms together. "So...are we doing this?"

"I wish I had the final say but I don't. I'm not gonna stand in his way."

"If Vincent comes along, safety is my top priority. It will be Havoc's too." He placed a hand on his chest to swear it.

Yeah right. Even when Havoc liked you, being around him was about as safe as holding a lightning rod in a storm. "Good luck telling them what to do."

"Thank you, I'll need it."

"Hey, I need you to do something for me." Lochlan had been looking for the right time to bring this up, and maybe now Maynard would understand that he owed Vince a little appreciation. "Can you stop being so formal around him?"

Maynard pursed his lips, as if he already knew what Lochlan was getting at. "What do you mean?"

Lochlan rolled his eyes. "You keep calling him 'Vincent,' like he's a stranger. He's your roommate. He's my husband. And because you and I are tied at the waist, he's kind of your husband too."

Maynard swayed like a shy little kid. A total rejection of nicknames was one of his weirder quirks and one only Lochlan's sister Joan appreciated. It wasn't until Candy cried that her Uncle Maynard 'didn't love her' that he finally stopped calling her 'Candace' and every time 'Corinne' came out of his mouth, Cori hit him with that you-are-so-old-and-embarrassing stare until it finally broke down his self-esteem.

Maynard smiled. "I promise I will consider calling him...not Vincent. At least, it's better than what Havoc has been calling him."

Lochlan cocked an eyebrow. "Which is?"

As punishment, Maynard actually bit his tongue. He pulled his comm to his face. It was completely silent when he said, "My timer is going off! The...bonding on your arm should be...I have to check on that now."

"I don't hear shit. Pierce?! Maynard!"

Half a box of fish fingers, a bulk bag of broccoli, and a frozen hunk of blueberries. Lochlan scrounged around the freezer, looking for anything to eat. With all of his energy officially spent, he planned on phoning it in for dinner anyway, but his options were looking about as generous as Sterillis III.

"Your arm is ready," Maynard announced, entering the kitchen to wash his hands. "Do you want to do calibration after dinner?"

"Sounds good." Lochlan knocked over an empty box that used to contain frozen samosas. "Hey, didn't we go shopping before we left Earth?"

Maynard came to the freezer and looked inside. "Yes? Of course we—goddamn it." He swung open the pantry and pushed aside an open bag of flour. He glowered and Lochlan could see it spelled in the wrinkles of his face: 'This is your fault.' As if Lochlan's elopement could also explain the other dozen times they put off grocery shopping.

Maynard started pulling random items out. "There has to be something we can make with...evaporated milk and multigrain bread?"

"Wait, hold on. Havoc's dinosaur chicken nuggets, your fancy cheese, and this tomato soup which is..." Lochlan turned the jar over to find the label. "Still in date! Hey, how's pizza?"

"Sounds...like heartburn but edible." Maynard turned the oven on to preheat.

"Look at that. You're not the only ideas-man." Lochlan scooped the slapdash ingredients in his arm and threw them onto the counter.

"I'll thank you if this doesn't send me into cardiac arrest."

Lochlan shoved him. "Chain smoking motherfuck-er."

With a laugh, Maynard pulled the sheet pan from the cabinet. "When this is over, we'll make a stop."

Lochlan headed into the hall toward his bedroom and braced himself. Vince hadn't said a word since their argument this afternoon, and since then, he'd been hiding out. God only knows what kinds of feelings he'd been stewing over. Now Lochlan had to tell him what they were having for dinner.

A sharp metallic noise made him jump. He looked over at clamoring from inside the elevator. When the doors opened, out tumbled Havoc and Vince.

"We're home, bastards!" Havoc stood to take a wobbly bow, arms fanned like a bargain-bin magician.

Climbing Havoc like a rope, Vince covered their mouth. "Shhh! Havoc, I don't want anyone to know that I'm drunk," he said at full volume in front of everyone.

"What did you do?" Lochlan asked Havoc.

They put a hand on their chest. "Me? Your precious husband made me suck tequila through a straw! He's the devil!"

Vince snickered into their shoulder and put a hand over their mouth. "I tried to warn them," he sang.

Oh, this was just unfair. A serious conversation was off the table for tonight. With no chance to clear the air, Lochlan had no chance of making a move on Vince, charming, funny, and a little flushed with liquor.

"By the way!" Havoc stumbled forward and poked a bony finger into Lochlan's chest. "He has options, so you better watch yourself, codger!"

Vince pulled them back, drowsily clinging to their arm. "Thank you, Havoc." He hiccuped. "You're so nice."

Lochlan could just pinch himself. "What the fuck am I looking at?" he asked Maynard, gesturing at the sloppy duo.

Havoc grabbed Vince by the shoulders and squared up to face him. "Listen, if it doesn't work out with Lochlan...you can stay with me and Maynard. We'll be good to you. Maynard, tell him!"

"And where am I going to go?" Lochlan asked.

"To hell where you belong!" Havoc tripped over their own heel to wag a finger in Lochlan's face.

With teary eyes, Vince shielded Lochlan. "But Havoc, I love him!"

"You can be our husband now! Right, May?"

"Good lord." Maynard dusted cheese off himself and rushed toward the group. "Havoc, my love. Let's lie down."

"Maynard doesn't want to marry me!"

"Of course he does!" Havoc said. "Are you kidding?"

With a mortified expression, Maynard mouthed, 'I'm so sorry' to Lochlan. Either Havoc had shapeshifted or they were simply too drunk to use their bones, but Maynard gave up on trying to get them to walk and flung them over his shoulder like a sack.

"You and the lubber, always pushing everyone around! I'm my own person too, dammit!" Havoc slurred to Maynard's back, kicking the air.

"That's nice, dear."

Weird. Lochlan felt a sudden weight against his torso; Vince's feathery hair hid his expression as he nuzzled into his husband's side.

"Loch...."

Weird, but nice.

"Come on. Let's get you to bed too." Lochlan eased Vince onto himself before carefully carrying him to their room.

With his elbow, Lochlan tapped on the door's entry pad. Starlight coming in through the glass wall allowed him to climb the steps without turning the lights on.

He set Vince down on the edge of their bed and then retrieved his husband's pajamas from the drawer and returned just in time to catch Vince teetering back toward the steps. "Hey." He spun Vince around and back toward their bed. Vince persisted, pushing off and aiming for the steps. "No. This way." Lochlan sat him back down. Vince blew a sharp breath at his bangs. He wadded himself in their comforter and dragged it with him as he continued his march for the stairs. "Where are you going?" Lochlan asked, stepping in front of him.

"I'm sleeping on the couch! Move." Vince attempted to charge past again.

"The hell you are! Sit still." Cushioned fists pummeled Lochlan as he defended the stairs. Even with one arm, he easily kept Vince in place. A funny but horrifying picture of this on a battlefield formed in Lochlan's mind.

"You don't tell me what to do!"

"I'm not—fuck!" Lochlan grabbed Vince's shoulder; he nearly slipped past. "Vinni, just sit the hell down!" Lochlan forced Vince to walk backward into bed.

"Fine! But only because this made me dizzy...." Vince finally sat down, head bobbing on his shoulders like ice in a drink.

Lochlan crouched, now eye level with his swaying husband. "What is going on with you?" He stretched an arm across Vince's side, half wanting to hold him, half wanting to block him from running off again. "I don't like that. I don't care how mad you are at me. We sleep in the same bed."

"I just wanted some space."

"No, you don't. What? Two weeks wasn't enough?"

Fine. Havoc and Maynard had a point. Lochlan should have waited. He should have, he just couldn't. When he hopped in the shuttle bound for Vegas, he wasn't thinking with his brain, but his friends were wrong if they thought he was thinking with his dick. It was his idiot heart that was to blame for his idiot behavior. And right now his heart was telling him it wasn't fair to whisk Vince away from his entire world just to leave him alone for days on end.

Lochlan sighed. "Vinni, listen. I've been thinking about what I want to say. Just give me a second to get it out the right way, okay?"

Vince stared at Lochlan, his expression shifting. He took Lochlan's hand. "I'm listening."

"I know how amazing you are. I do know that and I do care. You don't have to prove anything to anyone. Especially not me. But, that thing on the station is dangerous. Look at me." He raised his arms to present one lost, and the other decked in scars. "This is the job. This is what it looks like. If anything happened to you, I couldn't live with myself."

"Loch...." Vince rubbed his husband's shoulders. "I keep telling you that you don't need to worry about me. I'll be fine."

"You don't know that!"

"Well, how do you think I feel?" Vince held Lochlan's head so he could look him in the eye. "Do you think you're invincible? Because—speaking as an expert—you're not." He pressed his forehead to Lochlan's. "I was so worried the entire time you were gone, and I kept thinking I'd feel better if I were there. I could protect you."

"You want to protect me?" It was always Lochlan's instinct to be the shield. It never occurred to him that anyone would want to be his.

Vince rubbed the sides of Lochlan's jaw. "I know how I look, but I'm not made of glass, I promise. Actually, a very handsome and powerful man once compared me to the prom queen of horror."

Vince didn't need magic to charm. His sweet tequila breath and the hypnotic reassurance in his eyes were a force to be reckoned with. Lochlan still had his doubts, but he couldn't bring himself to say no. Not when Vince held him like this.

"...Fine." Lochlan said with a heavy groan. "Help us out this one time, but swear to me, at the first sign of trouble, and you are out of there."

Vince brightened up, stars twinkling around his crown. He wrapped his arms around Lochlan's neck, showering him with kisses. "On my life! *Mi cielo*, I promise this is going to be the best decision you've ever made!"

Despite Lochlan's frown, the kisses chipped away at his resolve. "Maybe after marrying your stubborn ass. Get in bed," he grumbled.

Vince bit his lip, tugging Lochlan over himself. "Say that again...slower."

Hunger replaced the annoyance on Lochlan's face. The couple was long overdue for some one-on-one time. For Lochlan, the best way to work through tension was to sweat it out.

With no will to resist the pull, Lochlan whispered in Vince's ear. "Get. Your ass. In Bed."

A New High
Chapter 14

Finally. Vince's mind slipped away when Lochlan's hand found its way up his thigh.

While it had only been a couple of days for Lochlan, a whole two weeks was an impossible amount of time to wait for Vince. Most newlyweds were venereous, of course. But the combination of Vince's over-energized magic condition and Lochlan's appetite meant the couple had been at it almost every day since their first time. Sometimes twice a day, but if anyone asked, they were doing it a perfectly healthy amount. Then again, the average Chorister priest might consider even once an unhealthy amount. It didn't matter. It wasn't Vince's fault that Lochlan looked like a Greek God and was good with his hands.

Vince hurried to unbutton his shirt in pace with his husband trailing ravenous kisses down the length of his torso. With each kiss, pulses of wild magic forced him to shiver, but he kept it tamed. His breath hitched when Lochlan's muscular hand rubbed his hardening cock over his pants.

Vince rushed his fingers up Lochlan's shirt. He let them fall onto Lochlan's back and massaged the muscles along the spine; it felt tense. That could just be the excitement, but Vince couldn't relax if he didn't know for sure. "How's your back?" he asked.

Lochlan hardly let his mouth stay off of Vince long enough for a proper breath. "Uh. It's fine," he panted. Which obviously meant it wasn't.

Vince hated to, but he pulled Lochlan off his torso. "Come here." He channeled some of his excess energy into a deep kiss laced with a trace of healing magic. The high that passed between their lips was light, but Lochlan chased the kiss as if he were addicted to it. As he pressed their tongues together, his irises expanded and his muscles loosened. A dreamy fog blurred their vision.

"That feels amazing...." Lochlan kissed Vince's neck and between pecks he whispered, "But nothing feels better than you."

Vince shared the feeling about his husband. He tore off the shirt and pants constraining him. Lochlan positioned himself between Vince's legs. It was so thrilling to see the taller man on his knees—even more thrilling when he softly mouthed at Vince's shaft over his boxers. Vince did not push back his gasps, shamelessly delighting in the swells of warmth caused by hot breath. Lochlan gripped Vince's hip, moving to kiss underneath his testicles.

He slipped his thumb beneath the elastic of Vince's boxers. With verdant eyes sparkling in the starlight, he teased, "More?"

"Yes," Vince sighed. He wanted Lochlan everywhere. It shouldn't have surprised him, but he was so hard he couldn't stand it. When Lochlan removed the underwear, Vince's dick twitched in demand for more touch. Lochlan generously peppered it with soft kisses, and the stubble of his chin lightly scratched the inside of Vince's thighs. Lochlan repeated the motions from before, making his way toward Vince's bottom. He was so close to the hole it made Vince squirm. "More, Loch."

"Yes, sweetheart." His low growl rumbled against Vince's groin. He stood. Wrapping his large hand around the thigh, Lochlan tugged Vince down to line his ass up with the edge of their bed. "You're gonna have to help me out here." He chuckled, pulling over a small red pillow. Vince tucked the cushion under his back to prop himself up. "That's my boy," Lochlan praised. He held his thumb to Vince's lips, and Vince understood. He sucked Lochlan's finger, coating it completely. Lochlan hummed in approval when Vince ran his tongue up the length of his finger, and when he felt satisfied, he pulled away. Vince gripped his own thighs, spread his legs apart, and pulled them as close to his chest as possible. He couldn't help but blush at the position. Lochlan brought his thumb down to the furl of muscle. Vince tensed up as Lochlan began massaging and kissing his bottom, circling the rim.

Stars conjured in a halo around Vince, and before long, he was a whimpering mess, praying for more sensation. A ravished smirk fixed on Lochlan's face. He sat back, taking in the sight of Vince crying for him and rubbing his cock against Vince's thigh. He was perfect. Bright and warm, he fell over Vince like the sun over the Earth, and the homesickness faded. They could be anywhere in the universe. As long as they were together, Vince was happy.

Lochlan crouched to lay his slobbering tongue flat against Vince's hole. He knew exactly how to move, making achingly slow and broad strokes. The pleasurable rhythm forced Vince into elated moans. A few spontaneous stars circled the couple.

Vince laced his fingers into Lochlan's hair, arching into the tongue and earning himself a delicious-sounding grunt of excitement from his husband. Gods, he really missed this.

"*Dámelo.*"

"Fuck, you sound so good." Every so often, Lochlan's stunning emerald gaze latched onto Vince. Every time his face appeared, he looked more wound. With a coiled expression ready to burst, he reached out to the nightstand, yanked the drawer open, and shoved the contents inside around. He grew agitated at how long it was taking to find the lubricant, knocking things off the table. Vince continued to enjoy the work of Lochlan's tongue, feeling a sense of karmic justice for making him wait so long.

Lochlan's tap on Vince's thigh signaled he'd found the bottle. Vince sat up to help, but Lochlan had beaten him to it, nimbly working the bottle with only one hand. He slathered his palm with lube and brought it to his own erection.

Vince sat up on his elbows, appreciating the view of Lochlan's shoulder moving up and down, stroking his own shaft and the bobbing of fluffy white hair as he continued rimming. With each lap, Vince gripped the sheets more fiercely. He was inching toward the edge now but trying to contain himself. He cried out a string of sweet obscenities as Lochlan stiffened his tongue to make quick circles around the outside.

As fantastic as it felt, Vince needed more. "Loch. Please. I really miss your cock." No hesitation. At the cue, Lochlan stood and swiped the bottle again. Vince motioned for his husband to slow down with an outstretched hand. "No, no. You lay back," he said breathlessly. "You deserve this."

He sat up, positioned Lochlan to lean against their headboard, and straddled his husband's lap. The thick throbbing vein on Lochlan's cock signaled a craving for Vince's warmth. Loosely, Vince wrapped his hand around the shaft, gliding it up and down to slick it with more lubricant.

Lochlan rasped when Vince's hand twisted firmly, a trace of pre-come trickling out. "Oh." A playful smile touched Vince's lips as he watched his husband's passionate show. "For me? Thank you, Loch. That's very sweet of you."

Lochlan grabbed a fistful of Vince's hair. The slight pain caused him to shudder. Lochlan brought his mouth to Vince's ear and growled, "God, you are so fucking gorgeous." His deep rumble forced a shiver down Vince's spine. He was strong enough to restrain both of Vince's hands in his one and breathed deeply to manage his own excitement.

Vince felt like he should wait too. He didn't want to come too soon, but with Lochlan himself looking more glorious than anything in the universe, the tight grip had the opposite effect. He couldn't stop himself from begging, "Lochlan, please...."

"So sweet," Lochlan murmured, kissing along Vince's neck.

"Loch, pretty please?" Vince keened. Right at the sweet spot, Lochlan bit down hard on Vince's neck. "Lochlan!"

Lochlan's lips curved into a smirk. "I love it when you say my name like that." He placed his hand on Vince's hip. "Sit up, sweetheart." Vince obeyed. At least in their bedroom, Lochlan could get him to do anything. Bracing onto his husband's shoulder, Vince leaned forward and lined up Lochlan's cock with his hole. "Breathe. Nice and slow," Lochlan reminded.

Vince nodded. By now, he was more used to Lochlan's size, but it was best not to be overconfident. Encouraged, Vince slowly lowered himself, breathing deeply. Lochlan stifled a moan with every movement. His voice was always such a turn-on, but these velvety grumbles were testing Vince's patience. Coming down too fast, Vince jolted at an awkward stretch.

Lochlan froze. "You okay?"

"Yes! Ah...I just really missed you," Vince huffed out a laugh.

"Well, it's not like I'm going anywhere." Lochlan shut Vince up with a kiss before he could come back. "What color's the light, baby?"

"Green. Very, very green."

He continued lowering himself onto his husband. After a torturous amount of time, he fit the entire length. With his head tilted back and breaths heavy, Lochlan waited for permission to move. Slowly, Vince swayed his hips to show it was okay. Lochlan wrapped his arm around Vince and gently rocked into him, checking often before moving faster.

Pleasure overcame Vince. He savored Lochlan's soft grunting, handsome expression, and fierce eye contact. As Vince's excitement grew, so did the magical feeling inside him.

"That's it, baby, you're taking it so well."

Gradually, Vince picked up the pace with swears and moans. Vince understood Lochlan's firm grasp of his ass as a cue to change his rhythm. In slowing down or speeding up, Vince tried to keep the ride going as long as possible. Lochlan surprised him with a spanking.

"Fuck, Loch!"

"You feel amazing, Vino. Keep going."

The tattooed glyphs on Vince's chest and back began glowing. Light engulfed his eyes. Shifting his hands from Lochlan's shoulders, Vince gripped the head-board behind them. Lochlan squeezed a hand around Vince's cock, stoking it in tandem with their thrusts. The sensation made it impossible for Vince to hold on to the concentration needed to suppress his magic. Stars conjured all around him, spilling out of his skull with a high-pitched shimmer like glass rain. "Así, amor, así."

Knowing how easily Vince's magic could latch on and drain his energy, Lochlan leaned back but didn't let up on his thrusting. His willingness to risk it all just for the pleasure of fucking his husband only further aroused Vince, who was finding it harder and harder not to come.

"You're so good to me, sweetheart. I'm almost there." After a few more hard thrusts, Lochlan finished first, but he pushed through it for a few more seconds.

When Vince came, a burst of energy forced its way out of his hand. The magical push detached the bed from its headboard, causing the frame to levitate momentarily before it collapsed. With Vince still on top, Lochlan shouted as he fell back into the newly made cavern between the bed and headboard.

The couple paused, taking a moment to process what had happened. Their eyes met, and they burst into laughter. In their blissful bubble, the rest of the world melted away.

Vince wiped back tears of joy. Still lying, Lochlan let out a pained, "Ack...my back," clutching at it.

"Oh, no!" Vince stayed perfectly still. "Are you okay? I'm so sorry!"

"I'm alright, just help me up...." Lochlan reached up. Vince stood and tried to bolster his massive husband to his feet, but all he managed was to help Lochlan fall into bed. "We'll move this back tomorrow. I'm exhausted."

"I'll take care of this then?" Vince poked the cybernetic leg. Lochlan nodded. Less reluctantly than before. Taking the leg off went smoother for Vince this time, and he did it mostly by himself. With time, his confidence would improve. Hopefully.

He set the leg into the charger and settled into bed next to his husband. "I didn't throw your back out, did I, old man?"

"No. I'm like a tank." Lochlan beat on his chest.

"Sure. Totally invincible." Vince kissed Lochlan's cheek, laid his head on his chest, and traced doodles on his pec. He would have pushed for another round, but he wasn't feeling so invincible tonight either. "Hey, Loch?"

"Vino." Lochlan's eyes remained shut, but he rubbed Vince's back to show he was listening.

"I know it's like, your job to throw yourself at giant space vacuums or whatever, but you know I couldn't take it if something happened to you, right?"

Lochlan squeezed Vince a little tighter. "Yeah."

"I know I should be more supportive, but I'm not. In fact, I'm going to be really selfish and say that you have to be here. For me. No matter what, your priority is coming home in one piece. You took an oath, and just because we swore it to an Elvis impersonator doesn't make it any less serious."

"Oh no. That makes it *way* more serious. I can't let the king down." His tone suggested the snarky look he probably had. "It's a deal."

Vince poked his husband's stomach, ordering him to repeat, "I, Lochlan Murdock...."

"I, Lochlan Murdock..." he paused to recall the phrasing. "Take thee, Vincent Luque, to be my husband, to have and to hold from this day forward, in good times and in bad, in sickness and in health, until death do us part. I promise to love and cherish you all the days of my life...and to give as many days to you as I can."

The newest addition to the vow forced a teary-eyed smile out of Vince. He kissed his husband's chest and closed his eyes. "To the edge of the universe and beyond." Vince was on the verge of the best sleep he'd had in almost two weeks.

Breakfast Breakdown

Chapter 15

//Vince

Eggs, pancakes, hash browns. "That should be good, right?" Vince fanned himself over a hot stove, pushing potatoes around on a pan.

The setup looked appetizing enough; American-style breakfast dishes haloed by the most adorable starbursts decorating the edges of milk glass. Gods, he loved this kitchen.

As if carried on the scent of smokey bacon and maple syrup, Lochlan entered the kitchen and nuzzled right up to Vince. "Morning, pretty boy." He kissed the top of Vince's head.

"Good morning, gorgeous." Vince leaned into his husband. After their romantic evening, Lochlan crashed as if he'd been the one out drinking all night.

"What's all this for?" He was practically drooling.

"I'm hungover and I cannot eat cereal again." Vince had cereal every morning since he moved in and this evening's mission called for proper fuel. "It would be rude to use up all your groceries without making some for everyone so eat your fill."

Lochlan turned a serving dish around and looked at it as if he'd never seen it before in his life. "We don't *have* any groceries."

Vince waved him away with the spatula. "You guys have plenty." This morning he woke early to re-organize the crew's total disaster they had going on in the pantry. No wonder they couldn't find anything to eat.

"Where can I get whatever the hell makes you so energetic?" Lochlan asked. Vince answered by ladling spiced coffee into a mug and handing it to his husband with a peck on the cheek. "Well. Now I can do anything."

"Good morning all," Maynard entered the room with a yawn and stretch. His eyes darted away from the cuddled up couple.

With a playful nudge, Vince elbowed Lochlan away. "Good morning, Maynard. How do you like your eggs?"

Maynard shot Lochlan a confused look, then replied, "Fried? Over easy, please."

"He wants them poached." Havoc stepped out from behind Maynard, arms folded as they approached the stovetop and squinted into the pan. His eyes sparkled with interest even as he seemed to grill the eggs.

Vince smirked. "Havoc. Would you like breakfast too?"

A finger tapped Havoc's chin with a skeptical flourish. "Hmmm, I'm not sure...are you food safety certified?"

Lochlan sat. "I watched you eat a fistful of sand once."

"Ew!" Vince shook the disgust off himself like sand out of a towel.

"Sunny side up it is!" Havoc chirped.

Vince bumped them with his hip. "Sit down. You are stressing me out."

Preceded by a shrug, Havoc spun on their heel and headed for the table, plopping into the seat between Maynard and Lochlan, who reacted with astonishment. Vince could only guess they had expected more of a fight from Havoc. After preparing scrambled eggs to his and Lochlan's liking, Vince served breakfast to the group.

"This looks delicious. Thank you, Vincent." Maynard's wide eyes could be mistaken for one of the plates in front of him.

"Oh, it's really nothing." With a coy wave of the hand, Vince brushed aside the compliment, but he wouldn't have been upset if Maynard carried on.

A mouthful of food muffled Lochlan as he picked up a bottle. "We had maple syrup?"

"It's almost out of date, so be generous. When was the last time you guys went shopping?" Maynard hunched over sheepishly. Lochlan shoved food in his mouth so he couldn't answer, and Havoc simply ignored the question.

Vince shook his head, completely disillusioned by the hardened and shipshape crew of spacers he'd experienced so far. When all was said and done, they were just like any other clueless group of guys. "How is it?"

"So good!" was the unanimous response.

Vince sat a little taller this morning. His roommates' cheerful reactions to his cooking completely distracted him from eating. With each satisfying bite, they leaned forward, hummed, and closed their eyes. The meal went quickly for everyone but him.

Lochlan finished first. He stood and pressed a kiss to his husband's temple, said, "Thank you, Vino," and made way for the dishwasher.

Maynard wiped his mouth and tossed the napkin onto his plate. "I hope this wasn't too much trouble."

"Not at all. I love cooking."

Maynard leaned forward on his elbows. "How did you learn?"

Vince gave a surprised smile; Maynard had never asked him anything about himself. "I always got stuck with cooking duty at the monastery. It kind of sucked at first because I was so bad. They make a big deal of meal times. We say that cooking is the first form of magic."

"What a charming way to trick children into doing their chores," Havoc teased.

Vince laughed. You could make that case for most of the monastery's rules. "Honestly, I think I just liked the alone time. I could sneak my music player and head-phones under my shirt."

Lochlan pointed out, "Now that sounds more you."

"Yup. Just me and Selena serving up lunch. I was pretty grateful I knew how to cook by the time I moved out." Vince had Maynard's full attention until Lochlan stepped toward the hallway.

Maynard sat up. "Lochlan, we still need to calibrate your arm."

Lochlan froze, sending a worried glance in Vince's direction. "Ah. Alright."

"The arm is ready?" Vince was impressed that the turnaround was so quick, but it was Maynard's design afterall. "Can I see it?"

Maynard seemed happy that Vince was curious. He opened his mouth to reply, but Lochlan cut in first. "Nothing to see. I'm putting it on now and we'll be right back."

"Actually, Lochlan...." Maynard walked over to him. They whispered to each other. Lochlan kept peeking over his shoulder. Vince stared at Havoc for a hint. With an eyeroll, Havoc threw their napkin down and strode over, overtaking the conversation.

Lochlan threw his arm in the air. "Okay, okay!"

Maynard turned back around, hands behind his back. "Vincent, join us."

"Just remember that everything is fine," Lochlan held his forearm parallel with the ground.

Vince should have given those expiration dates a quadruple-check. He nodded slowly, with a sinking feeling in his stomach. "Okay...I'm feeling great about whatever this is."

The lab was cursed. Definitely cursed. That was Vince's professional opinion. But he was trying to be nice.

Maynard made his own kind of mortal magic here. An iron grate separated the two levels of the room; the top level seemed reserved for record-keeping. Boxes, files, and binders filled tall shelves that lined the walls from floor to ceiling. At the very least, Vince found that part of the room charming;the way the older man showed an appreciation for analog despite his techy background.

The famous tower. During their night out, Havoc complained that Maynard was so married to his work that the lab 'might as well be our bedroom.' If Vince was remembering the layout correctly, the spiral staircase on the upper level should lead to the other couple's bedroom above.

On the bottom level, where the crew had gathered, Maynard's tools were precision mounted on the wall. Maybe they shone for him but they hit Vince's senses like oncoming headlights and he found himself dazed in the hospital-like set.

The clinical lighting was so stark everything looked unreal. Machines hummed, circling Lochlan like a surgical team. Reading the monitors did nothing to soothe Vince's nerves. They made no sense to him. Foot tapping, he watched Maynard secure the cybernetic arm onto a clamp and attach it to Lochlan.

After lowering a heavy-looking head-mounted lens over his glasses, Maynard reached for a pair of sharp tools. "Ready?" he asked.

Lochlan shifted in his seat and glanced back at Vince nervously. He gave a nod and said, "As I'll ever be."

With his foot, Maynard hovered over a pedal. "Disconnecting." He pressed the pedal down.

Lochlan jolted upright, like something had shocked him. His features twisted into knots as he pushed down painful groans.

Vince conjured an anxious pop of electricity and lunged forward, but Havoc placed a hand on his chest, urging him to sit back down. "He's fine," they yawned.

He didn't look fine. Vince had seen Lochlan run forehead first into a doorframe and not even blink. He grabbed hold of his necklace, tangling his finger in the chain. "So what's happening?"

Havoc folded their legs and leaned back in their chair. "Nothing. The arm connects to his brain, which is why we can't sedate him. Maynard says the process fires up all his nerve endings and Lochlan says it feels like being struck by lightning."

A dense aurora surrounded Vince. No spells then. In his hand, he gripped the pendant so tightly his fingers could have blistered. "Poor Loch...."

Lochlan writhed around, struggling to sit still. He muttered something under his breath. It was unnerving to see such a tortured expression across his brawny features.

"Lochlan, please try to hold still." Maynard's still face was the only anchor Vince had in this moment. The man who Lochlan claimed 'knew every damn thing' found no reason to worry. Vince tried to remind himself by looking at Maynard whenever he couldn't look at Lochlan.

"Fuck off," Lochlan snarled through gritted teeth.

Havoc patted Vince on the shoulder. "He says the yelling helps."

Unbothered, Maynard pointed a tool at the arm. "Reconnecting." Sparks flew out of it, and Lochlan struggled again not to wince.

"So dramatic." Havoc's expression was as indecipherable as always. Despite their cold words, they seemed focused on the scene.

The grating sound of a tool, paired with the visual of Lochlan writhing like an injured animal, turned Vince's stomach. He feared his husband might try to play it cool for his sake. If Vince wasn't there, would Lochlan let himself do whatever he needed to ease the pain? Maybe he should let the older man's ego win this time and step out of the room to give him some privacy.

It went completely against his nature to leave or to just sit there. He had the impulse to pray, but that felt more self-serving right now. Lochlan deserved the support he actually wanted.

"Can I do anything? Like, at all?" Vince asked. Havoc did not answer, still watching the scene like they were waiting for something.

Maynard paused and lifted his lens. "Lochlan, breathe. Do you need a break?"

Drenched in sweat, Lochlan croaked, "Just a sec." With a shake, he waved Havoc over. Immediately they stood and brought Lochlan a water bottle from a cooler beside them. Lochlan chugged it and threw it on the ground. Maynard and Havoc nodded at each other before the work continued.

As the machine fired back on Havoc, remained at Lochlan's side. "I crashed the shuttle," they said. Vince checked his ears to make sure he had heard that right.

"What?!" Lochlan threw his head back to scowl at them.

Havoc swayed side-to-side. "Yep, right into a lamppost. Last night." Vince's sorrowful aurora shifted into a rain of fire as he resisted the impulse to ignite Havoc. How could they kick Lochlan while he was already down? "Vince was there, he saw the whole thing." Havoc pointed a thumb in Vince's direction and Lochlan looked more disappointed than angry. Which was worse. Way worse.

Mierda. Vince shrunk into his seat as the evening flooded back to him. Note to self: never drink with Havoc.

"I'm gonna kill you!" Lochlan slammed on the stainless steel worktable with his fist.

Maynard jumped back, hot tool still in use. "Watch it!"

"Oh, it's only one little headlight. It still works!" Havoc fanned the singed arm.

"Dead! You are fucking dead—Jesus Christ!" Lochlan suddenly keeled over in pain.

"And!" Havoc grabbed Lochlan's head to face him away from the arm. "*And* I got a ticket." Vince covered his face. It was too much to take right now. He wished he could hide, but there was nowhere these harsh lights couldn't reach.

"Serves you right! They should have hauled your bony ass to jail!"

"Oh, I used your license. Did you know you have a warrant out for your arrest? Luckily, we're out of the jurisdiction for that."

Vince snapped, stomping over to yank Havoc out of the room. "What the hell is wrong with you?!" With a finger to his lips, Havoc shushed Vince and pointed towards Lochlan.

Lochlan's eyes and lips remained shut. He breathed shallowly through his nose; he showed a flicker of discomfort, but mostly he seemed preoccupied. "You're gonna pay for the repair with money or with blood. I mean it this time," Lochlan said, gripping his thigh.

Whatever Havoc was doing, it was working. They waved Vince to come closer, handed him a cloth rag from the cooler, and motioned for him to care for Lochlan.

"Oh…oh!" Vince dabbed the cool cloth to his husband's forehead. "Uhm, Loch, baby, don't be too mad, okay?" He checked with Maynard, who nodded to reassure him this was fine. "It was just an accident. Everything is okay," Vince lulled. The emotional whiplash seemed to work. Lochlan sighed, easing into Vince's touch.

Havoc put a hand on their hip. "Exactly. I mean, how was I supposed to know I parked in a fire zone?"

"Well, there was a big sign. You know, the one that said 'No Parking Fire Zone'?" Vince gently dabbed the sweat off Lochlan's neck.

"Dumbass," Lochlan spat.

Havoc rolled their eyes. "I can't drive *safely* if I'm *reading*."

Vince massaged Lochlan's shoulders, the tense muscles turned into putty in his hand. "Well, did you have to use Lochlan's license?"

"Yes. I'm not allowed to drive a shuttle."

Vince blanched. He couldn't have understood that correctly. This had to be Lochlan being possessive over his stuff. "What do you mean by that?"

"According to Lochlan, I'm 'bad at driving' and according to the law, I'm 'a threat to public safety.' Ridiculous."

"You better be joking! What did you do to get your license taken away?!" Vince shouted, feeling the flames of magical heat on his hands.

"I turned into a hamster," they answered flatly. Vince just stared at him in disbelief. "I was screaming, and I let the yoke swing me around! It was funny!"

"The officer didn't think so," Lochlan said. On hearing his voice, Vince snapped back into the moment and continued massaging.

"Oh, whatever," Havoc puffed. "What do they know about driving anyway? Lane hogs never use their signals or obey the speed limit!"

Lochlan rubbed his forehead. "Neither do you."

"Yet, they have a license, and I do not. Where is the justice?"

Lochlan bounced his head from side to side. "Well, you got a point there."

"*No!*" Vince shook Lochlan, channeling all his frustration into the massage. "Havoc, you should have *told me* you didn't have a license before I let you fly!"

Lochlan squeezed Vince's hand on his shoulder, signaling him to stop shaking him. "Hey. Go easy on them Vinni, it's not their fault the law is stupid."

Vince scoffed. "*Most* of the time, yes, but safety measures are different! I would *love* to take you both on a trip to any morgue or cemetery, and then we'll see how 'stupid' traffic rules are."

"And we're done!" Maynard powered down the machines, lifted his lenses, and rolled his chair back.

"Oh, thank goodness." Vince's legs gave way. Lochlan maneuvered him to collapse onto his lap. Havoc and Maynard's smooth work made him almost forget what was going on, but the second reality struck, the stress turned his bones into gelatin. "I thought I was gonna pass out. Oh! Loch, *mi bebe! ¡Pobrecito!* How are you?" Vince moved the hair stuck to Lochlan's sweaty brow and showered his husband's salty face in kisses.

"I'm okay, sweetheart." Lochlan's laughter was more fried than usual.

"Good job, everyone. Thank you." Maynard took a small bow and gestured to Lochlan, as if giving him the stage. Lochlan rotated his arm, flexed, and wiggled his fingers to show off the solid connection. "Excellent. Take a rest. We'll meet back after lunch." Maynard clapped twice, and the intense overhead lighting switched to a softer scene. The cool jazz coming from his headphones now played over the speakers. Stylish lamps and a holographic fireplace emitted a warm, attractive glow, transforming the lab from a cold hospital into an inviting study. Vince could now understand how Maynard could lose himself for hours in here, and maybe there was another reason he kept his bed so close by.

"So, what's for lunch?" Havoc asked. Vince peeled his sight from the gorgeous office to find everyone looking back at him.

With a contented smile, he replied, "I'll see what I can do."

The Mountain
Chapter 16

//Lochlan

Lochlan had never been so spoiled. As soon as they got back to their room, Vince prepared him a highball, rubbed him down, and kissed just about every inch of his body. After the best nap of his life, Lochlan woke to a rich, mouthwatering scent carried over from the kitchen. When he got up to investigate, he found Vince's just as drool-worthy figure, standing over a hot pot of tomato and egg drop soup, a recipe he picked up from their favorite restaurant in Chinatown.

Vince had even brought cookies and tea into the War Room. Maynard fussed at first—something about how 'serious' they should take the briefing—but he took one bite of the best damn polvorón any of them had ever had and shut right up.

"Okay, you're officially fucking with me," Lochlan said. "What is it? Some magic, bottomless bag of ingredients?"

"It has to be a conjuration spell." Maynard broke a cookie in half and inspected it.

"Aw, Maynard. Did you do homework?" Vince teased. Maynard ducked behind his mug, allowing the hot tea to fog up his glasses. He shoved a few cookies into a napkin and surrendered his seat to Vince. Standing during briefings was the usual for him, pacing around while he rambled. "All of this stuff was just lying around. Full offense, your kitchen looks like raccoons organized it," Vince said. He took a seat at the round table.

Maynard cleared his throat. "Anyway. Thank you all for meeting with me. The current phase of our mission is purely intelligence gathering. This afternoon I'll fit Vincent for a suit, do a run-through of safety guidelines, and we'll head for the station. Once there, Vincent will attempt contact with Dr. F'vr and then we'll return to the ship as quickly as possible. Understood?" Everyone nodded. "Now, Vincent, as you are aware, there is a hostile creature on the station. So long as it remains behind the door, there is *no* active threat. However, before you officially agree to come down with us, we want you to understand exactly what to expect. Havoc?" Maynard held his arm out to the shapeshifter.

Havoc stood and stepped back. "Reminder, this turned our bodyguard's titanium arm into confetti." With a spin, they shapeshifted into the creature, screeching and clicking. They brought its vacuuming face as close to Vince as possible. Vince held his necklace in place as the force pulled his hair and shirt upward. Havoc returned to their original form and fell back into their seat, kicking their feet up on the table. "Ta-da!"

Lochlan drummed his fingers on the table. "So?"

Vince swallowed, centering his pendant on his chest. "Okay...that's not so bad."

Lochlan put a hand over Vince's. "It's not too late to say you want to stay home."

Vince pulled his hand away to fix his hair. "It's fine. Really."

"Nobody's gonna be mad at you."

"I said it's fine!"

"Are you nuts?" That wasn't supposed to be out loud. The question just popped out of Lochlan.

"Okay, fine, I'm out of here." Vince picked up the plate of cookies to take with him. All at once, Havoc crammed a few into their mouth while Maynard grabbed the plate and shot Lochlan a glare.

Lochlan rolled his chair out to block Vince from leaving. "No, no, no!" He moved his husband to place the cookies back on the table. "Okay, fine. It's fine. Pierce, stop harping on the guy! He says it's fine, jeez!"

"That's what I thought." Vince fed Lochlan a cookie and patted him on the head. His hostage negotiation skills were impressive enough.

Maynard took off after the meeting to fit the crew's special guest into a suit. After years of the same old styles, he was all too excited to have something new to work up. The rest of the crew stayed back to handle the real hard work of polishing off the plate of cookies.

Lochlan took a heavy gulp of his tea and sighed. He gave Havoc a puffed-up look. "So. You and Vinni."

"Are there more words in that sentence?" Havoc asked. Lochlan brought his elbows to the table. An iron-hot stare was all he needed to grill the confession out of them. He gave it some time and Havoc frowned. "Stop looking at me like that." Lochlan did not let up, even as they squirmed. "Oh, shut up!" Havoc threw a cookie down onto the plate and folded their arms.

"I told you, you'd like him."

"Well, it's true what they say: nothing is impossible. Even *you* might stumble into a good guess every now and then. What do you want? A cookie?" They held up the treat and waved it in the air.

Lochlan folded his arms behind his head and leaned back. "Just wanted you to hear you say I was right."

Havoc stood. "Well. Whatever he tells you, just remember we were drunk, and he hit his head pretty hard."

"What's that mean?"

Havoc did not answer. They snatched the last cookie from the plate and stuffed it into their mouth. They pointed to it, suggesting they couldn't answer while eating, and scurried out of the room. Lochlan followed them to the hall, but they were gone. They move so damn fast, they could even be in the vents by now.

Noticing the open lab door across the hall, he checked on Vince and Maynard. He leaned in the doorway watching them work. Vince had suited up in everything but the helmet.

When Lochlan first put on the suit, he hated it. It was restricting and hot but Maynard insisted they needed to wear them in environments where they couldn't confirm the conditions. He remembered the way fabric wedged between his joints with every little movement. Maynard beat himself up for weeks after a failed chase where a bandit escaped with a package they were meant to deliver. Lochlan's leg came unhooked and he couldn't reach inside the suit to fix it. Maynard only blamed himself, padded the cybernetic limbs, and changed the suit to keep Lochlan's prosthetics out while keeping oxygen in. By the time Havoc came along he'd learned a lot about making accommodations and made their suit especially stretchy so they could keep it on and shift into a wider range of species.

This time it seemed like Maynard really got the hang of things. He had a notebook filled with info on where and how magic built up in the body and a bunch of different materials laid out which Vince, of course, seemed to have extremely strong opinions on. *Third time's a charm.*

By the looks of it, Maynard planned to fix Vince's necklace to the outside of his suit and was working on specialty gloves. He added a bunch of extra pouches to the belt. Vince tucked a book of matches and a pocket-sized tome away while Maynard checked the fit of his pants.

"We usually collect plant samples in this," Maynard said, handing Vince a florafolio. He stared at the little pill-shaped, refrigerated container in his hand and popped it open to tuck a fresh marigold inside. When he closed it, an internal sprayer misted the flower.

Vince held up the container to the light and caught Lochlan staring. "How do I look?" He fanned his arms out to show the suit.

Instead of saying the suit looked like his worst nightmare, Lochlan said, "You look like the prettiest damn astronaut I've ever seen," and pulled in his husband for a kiss on the cheek.

"Haven't you seen yourself in a mirror?" Vince flashed his signature simper instantly muddling Lochlan's thoughts.

"Ahem. Trying to work." Maynard concentrated on sewing.

"You could probably take it in here, Pierce." Lochlan pointed at Vince's ass.

Vince gave him a playful shove. "Stop it!" He saw himself in the full-length mirror and turned to check himself out. "Wait. Could you?"

Maynard took his headphones from his desk and put them on. He cranked the music up so loud that it was audible from the outside. "Sorry, I can't hear you!" he said.

Vince laughed at Maynard, about to crack a joke before he saw Lochlan's face. His brow turned up. "Are you okay?" he asked and grabbed Lochlan's hand.

Lochlan guessed he hadn't done so well at masking his stress. He was trying to but seeing Vince in the suit made it all too real. "It's just hitting me."

"We'll be in and out." Vince kissed the back of Lochlan's hand. "Right?"

"Right." Lochlan returned the kiss with a squeeze.

He noticed that Maynard's music disappeared somewhere in the middle of their conversation. He looked at his best friend, who continued to pretend he wasn't listening but gave a reassuring nod as Lochlan left the room. It was probably safest for everyone to let them work in peace.

The crew, plus Vince, loaded themselves up onto the shuttle. Lochlan was happy to have his seat back. He caressed the dashboard, a small apology for letting other people get handsy with his Pim.

"Are you going to kiss?" Vince teased. "Should we leave?" Lochlan shot him a frown. Maynard and Havoc didn't even try to hide their laughter.

"You can get in line," Lochlan answered.

Maynard started the timer on their comms after he explained everyone should keep an eye out for any patterns in the time jump. While he usually preferred quiet time in the shuttle, he jabbered through most of the ride. "Again, the helmet needs to stay on at *all* times," he said.

"*Yes*, Maynard. Thank you for reminding me I need oxygen to breathe," Vince sighed.

While it was worth mentioning, Maynard had gone over it about a dozen times already. Meanwhile, Lochlan spent his ride with Elton John, drowning Maynard out and batting Havoc's hand away from the radio at the end of *every* song.

"Leave it!" Lochlan grabbed their wrist. "Even dogs know what that means."

Their fingers extended to click the screen's music app and change the song. "Look, I love sir Elton, but you always play the same songs! Vince and I want to listen to musicals. Isn't that right, Vinni?" Havoc gave Vince some kind of 'inside joke' look that he rolled his eyes at.

"Not this again," Maynard groaned. "Captain's privileges. Put on Billy Preston."

"What about driver's privileges? If either of you touch that dial, I'm gonna pop a hole in your suit."

Jokingly, Vince raised his hand. "Can I suggest something?" He sat forward to reach for the shuttle stereo and opened the search bar. "Kind of rock, kind of soul, kind of theater...."

Hearing the first notes of a Queen song on the stereo, Maynard and Lochlan looked at each other and burst into laughter. Vince hit the nail right on the head.

"Oh! I haven't heard this song in so long." Havoc whistled along when the vocals came in.

Maynard looked to the back seat. "Havoc, have we ever told you about the first time Lochlan and I saw them live?"

"Unfair. Gods, I wish I could have gone."

"Still can't believe I convinced Pierce to skip class."

Maynard cringed at the memory of the A, not A+, he received on their mid-term. "Don't remind me."

"Showing your age there, boys," Vince teased.

"Right," Lochlan and Maynard mumbled, equally sheepish while Havoc just elbowed Vince.

Maynard's bashfulness disappeared quickly, and he hummed out a short laugh. With a smug look he said, "You know...that was before Vincent was even born."

Lochlan punched him on the softest part of his arm. "Don't you start!"

"Ew!" Vince shriveled, looking like he could just slot himself between the seat cushions.

"Alright, everybody keep it down!" Lochlan turned up the music to drown out Havoc and Maynard's horrible laughter.

The rest of the ride was strangely peaceful. Everyone sang or hummed along with the music. Not one time did Maynard grab his head or plunge into his bag for medicine. Lochlan tried not to let himself relax too much—comfort usually came with just as much trouble—but, damn, this was nice. By the time he pulled into the station, he actually asked himself if things were going to be alright. After all the crap life had handed him this week, maybe he'd earned a little easygoing.

He switched the shuttle off and the magnets on. With a confident grin on his face, he turned around to find Vince in a haze of magical energy, shaking like a tree in a storm.

THE CHASM
CHAPTER 17

//Vince

Vince felt his stomach leap into his throat, taking all the moisture in his mouth as he swallowed it back down. He looked out into the infinite nothingness. Suddenly, he felt no larger than a speck of dry clay, the small stretch of space between the shuttle and the station like a canyon.

Lochlan, preparing to exit the vehicle, saw Vince, taut like sun-bleached leather, and asked, "Vinni? Are you alright there, honey?"

Vince gripped the seat. "H-hypothetical question. If I slipped, what uh...where would I go?"

"You'd just float forever in whichever direction you fell." Of course, Havoc would say something like that so casually.

"Forever? Like, forever, forever? Just out into the cold? To freeze to death?"

"Oh, don't worry. The suit is extremely well-made. Unless you crash into something, you'd die of starvation first." Maynard sounded far too proud of himself. When Vince gaped at him, he reeled off, "But try not to think about that! Mind your contact points, move slowly, and don't look out. Just focus on what you're touching."

Lochlan reached over the seat to place a firm, comforting hand on Vince's knee. "It's easier than it looks, Vinni. I swear, it's like moving through a pool."

The cool jade of Lochlan's eyes catching the star light brought Vince back to his center. The crew had done this hundreds, if not thousands, of times before. Surely, Vince could pull it off just once.

Me aviento. He knew he had to jump on that bravery while he had it. He took a deep breath, sat up confidently, and nearly choked when he looked just past Lochlan's beautiful head, out the window, into the gaping void again.

"...Is it too late to go home?"

The softness of Lochlan's gaze disappeared as he huffed, "Oh, no you don't. Not after all that fuss you made. Move your ass, Luque!" His no longer comforting hand grabbed Vince by his suit forcibly and yanked the smaller man forward.

"Lochlan! Lochlan, no!"

Lochlan used the tether from his suit to strap them together. He tossed Vince onto his shoulder and slammed on the button to open the tower. He climbed up the ladder with Vince over his shoulder and the crew behind him.

"Three. Two. One." The airlock turned from orange to blue. Vince's firm hold on Lochlan didn't prevent him from noticing their sudden weightlessness. Lochlan bounded up the ladder into space and now, a tether and a prayer were all that stood between Vince and a seven-day countdown to organ failure.

He kicked around in a panic. "Lochlan, I'm begging you! Put me down! This is a million times worse! I'll climb!"

"Will you quit squirming around? I'm gonna slip for real."

"Got it!" Vince squeaked.

He shut his eyes and held stiff as a board. The entire way down, Vince muttered prayers under his breath along with a hailstorm of damnations directed at his husband.

"I *heard* that," Lochlan gruffed, placing Vince down onto the station. "There you go," he heaved. Only after being shaken did Vince open his eyes. A wave of relief washed over him as sweet gravity took hold. He wanted to kiss the ground, but—as he'd been reminded so often—he needed oxygen to breathe. Instead, Vince clung to Lochlan, shaking and begrudgingly grateful for the push into the deep end. "You did great, Vino," Lochlan whispered, rubbing his back.

"And we hardly noticed you crying!" Havoc said.

Maynard checked the screen mirror he'd set up with the ship's computer on his comm. "The time on the computer is April 11th, almost 6pm."

Vince checked his own comm in disbelief. They'd arrived no longer than 5 minutes ago, but four hours had already passed in real time.

Maynard looked like he was searching for a thought, but gave up. "We need to move. Let's do a quick final-check."

Safe within the station, calmness settled over Vince, and his awareness of the surrounding spiritual energies heightened. He took one step forward, and suddenly a maelstrom of spiritual noise assaulted his senses. Many voices thundered and crashed over one another like a static-ridden storm.

"Hey." Lochlan noticed the pained expression on Vince's face and pulled him close.

Shaking his head, Vince forced his thoughts through the chaos. "I'm okay. Just trying to focus, but it's so noisy in here."

"What kind of noise?" Maynard held his comm out to record the response.

"It comes in like radio static, if that makes sense." Vince tuned in again, trying to discern voices from each other and glimpses of figures hanging just outside his peripheral vision. "There are...seven spirits tethered to the station."

Lochlan exhaled. "So nobody made it out." Vince couldn't help but pity the researchers. Even if they were kinda sketchy.

"Yeah. They're all here, and they're all *really* unsettled. I can't make out a thing. I need to move somewhere else." Vince headed down a quieter wing.

Allowing him to lead the way, the crew hung close behind. Maynard had already given Vince a rundown of the layout earlier. A supply closet should be a low-energy place.

On passing through the supply chamber, Vince noticed the large dark machine the crew had shown him a picture of. *A quantum tunneling device*, he recalled. A sudden, powerful force seized his attention. The torrent of emotions knocked Vince over, but Lochlan swooped in and caught him. Lochlan seemed on the verge of death himself, pale as a ghost. "What's wrong?" he asked.

Vince shivered, the icy push chilling him down to his bones as he tried to subside the mixed emotions he was picking up on. "I'm okay, Loch. I promise. It's just that the energy here is heavy and unstable. I got a little thrown off balance."

"So how's it feel?"

Vince had told Lochlan before about the layers between the living world and the Veil. The closer to the Veil Vince got, the more susceptible he became to the emotions of unsettled spirits, and these spirits were some of the most frenzied he'd ever come across.

"Scared mostly...and guilty. And *so* angry. Like, Gods, I feel like I could just...." Vince's vision went red hot, his muscles tensed and his breathing quickened, violent urges overtook his mind. Lochlan snapped Vince out of it. A bead of sweat trickled down his forehead. "Oh, now I'm sweating! Gross!"

"Vince!" Lochlan yanked Vince back up to stand. "I'm gonna send you back to the shuttle."

"O-oh, right!" Just like that, the rage vanished. Vince tried again to detect it, but only panic remained. "One spirit—a really angry one—is really difficult to get a read on."

"What do you mean?" Maynard typed the events in his comm.

"It's like it was here one second and then gone the next. I've felt that kind of anger before and...I don't think that the asteroid killed them. Not all of them." The crew gleaned the grim subtext of the theory, exchanging worried glances. "Can I see Dr. F'vr now?"

Maynard led him toward the corpse. The air chilled further as they approached the cold spot stemming from the body.

The signs of death were clearly present in Dr. F'vr: dull skin, warped posture, and glazed eyes. The crew reacted to the doctor with less concern than expected.

Though Vince didn't flinch at the corpse either, it still disturbed him with its remarkably fresh state. Six months with no signs of decomposition? The poor soul was not resting well.

Ignoring the crew's collective cringe, Vince knelt beside the doctor to test for rigor mortis. He closed Dr. F'vr's eyes, laid him flat on his back, and crossed his arms over his stomach. Vince tucked the marigold from the florafolio into the doctor's clasped hands. A force tugged at him again, and the cloud of Vince's breath was visible inside his helmet.

"Is it that cold?" Havoc asked.

Maynard circled him. "There's not an issue with your suit, is there?"

"No, this is a good thing. Dr. F'vr is definitely close by," Vince chimed.

"Oh!" Maynard jotted that down. "Great, so what happens now?"

Each of Lochlan's friends secured one of his hands on their shoulder. "You remember Halloween Horror Nights with the kids?"

Maynard raised a brow. "Yeah?"

Lochlan winked, then pulled the crew aside. "You're gonna love this." At least the easy-going tenor meant he was starting to relax.

With room to work, Vince started by taking a lighter out of his bag and removing the necklace latched onto the outside of his suit. The pendant's side latch opened, revealing the incense within. A sweet aroma of frankincense and myrrh filled the air as Vince ignited the resin. He lowered the mini-thurible over the doctor and closed his eyes.

"I pray in the name of the sovereign spirit of death, Xovivos. Xovivos, renew your spirit in me, keep my companions and I safe from harm, watch over our coming and going both now and forever more. *Así sea.*" Vince swung the thurible around to purify the space. "*Escúchame,*" he whispered. While everything remained the same for the crew, the simple spell carried Vince closer to the entrance of the Veil; close enough to be heard. The walls faded away, and the station overlapped with the darkness of the other world. "To those who tethered to this station or its articles, I am Vincent Luque. I am a...priest and a servant of the Veil. I invite those aboard who have a message for the living to communicate with me. I am requesting Dr. F'vr, but I welcome any spirits who wish to come forward." Vince kept ear out for faint voices popping through the static. The station remained quiet, and the static smooth.

"Well, this was a bust," Havoc said.

Vince didn't hold it against him. The crew couldn't feel what he could. Spirits, similar to humans, were often wary of unfamiliar voices in the dark.

"Dr. F'vr, if you're listening, there's no need to be afraid. I'd just like to pass on your message. I'll show myself now. *Mirame.*"

Vince's practice had given him an extraordinary gift–the ability to not only connect with spirits but also to move among them. When he assumed responsibility as the cathedral's necromancer, the church embedded his private entrance to the Veil into his skin. The inside of Vince's suit lit up, illuminated by the tattoos on his back and chest. When he opened his eyes, they rolled into the back of his head, glowing a solid white, something Lochlan said reminded him of a slot machine. The translucence of Vince's skin revealed parts of his glowing skeleton beneath. Finally, to separate him from the world of the departed, a sparkling, spectral veil shielded him.

Vince caught the sound of a wolf whistle in his direction, which he could only assume to be Havoc, as Lochlan was laughing.

"Right?" Lochlan said. "You look as pretty as our wedding day, sweetheart."

"Oh, stop," Vince giggled.

His rolled-back eyes made it unclear what he was looking at. He used the advantage to peek at the crew's reactions. Havoc and Lochlan grinned menacingly at Maynard as he nervously coughed and remained silent. Vince was too busy to pick that apart. Lochlan could fill him in later.

Because of the open Veil, those nearby could partially share the sight and sound. The crew jolted at the chime of a bell and the rise of Dr. F'vr's spirit above his corpse. Vince adored the way Lochlan reflexively pushed his friends behind him. "He's here. I'll be right back," Vince said.

His spirit stepped out of his body, leaving it behind so he could enter the threshold of the Veil. Gently, he sent his corporeal form to levitate in place and drifted into the darkness, away from the group.

As the station became a speck in the distance, a tunnel appeared ahead of him with a light shining on the other side. He passed through the long stretch of darkness and entered the desert.

In the desert between the living world and the Necropolis, Vince often found unsettled spirits wandering around. The serene nature was a calming welcome into the afterlife. Above a backdrop of mountains, twinkling stars dotted a lilac sky. Oases were frequent and plentiful, hugged by patches of lush vegetation. Beyond that, vibrant flowers peeked out of crackling brown clay. Gliding alongside a cool sparkling river, phantasmal fish and birds followed Vince everywhere he went.

The desert offered a place for rest and contemplation before continuing one's journey; however, some lingered, bound by unresolved issues in the living world. Looking for a chance to slip back through the curtain, spirits would turn the opposite direction of the city and become lost. This is where Vince came in. His position as necromancer swore him to guide those lost souls.

Today, he answered the call of a spirit burning with incompleteness. He found the doctor seated on a rock beside the water. Dr. F'vr approached, not looking like himself; so irresolute that his spirit was reduced to a wispy, featureless husk, only identifiable by the marigold tucked into his hand.

Dr. F'vr stood from the rock he sat on. "...Lu...que?" the voice crackled.

"Yes, that's me, Dr. F'vr. It's nice to meet you." Vince bowed his head in respect.

"You...hear...me?"

"Yes, I can hear you, but it's difficult, so please talk slowly. Can you tell me what happened to you?"

Dr. F'vr looked to the ground. "Accident..."

"I understand an asteroid hit the station, but that's not all that happened, is it?" Vince chose his words carefully. Spirits in such a state were vulnerable and easily confused.

The fading voice whispered, "Wasn't there...then...it was..."

A sudden surge of wrath caused Vince to lose concentration. He looked for the source and spotted another spirit, radiating the same violent energy as earlier, peering from behind a cactus. Just like before, the powerful emotion nearly knocked Vince over. He clung to a tree in the desert as a faded overlay of the station came into view. Dr. F'vr rose, startled by Vince's wavering presence.

Damn it. And Vince was doing so well. He couldn't lose concentration now. Not when he was finally starting to feel useful. How might Lochlan's friends see him if he couldn't complete the job after all the hype? He'd sooner jump into open space than go home and face the humiliation.

"I-I'm sorry, Dr. F'vr. It's very difficult to make out what you're saying. Would you like to come forward so I can hear you better?"

"Forward...." Dr. F'vr charged.

"Uh." Vince took a step back. "Just a *little* closer. But—chill out!" Dr. F'vr did not heed the warning. He collided with Vince, yanking off his veil. "No! Don't touch m—"

Get A Load of This Guy

Chapter 18

Maynard was almost offended that Lochlan had not revealed Vincent's skill sooner. His career afforded him the privilege of meeting a handful of spellcasters and he had seen magic before; a few flamboyant tricks impress an audience and ensure a good image, but this was different–horrifying and gripping. He typed the mission's progress into his comm with boyish enthusiasm.

If studied, a spellcaster's 'gift'—as they called it—could propel humanity decades into the future, but the vultures of religious hierarchy plucked individuals with the rare skill and bound them with rigid traditional practices. Part of that tradition meant keeping remarkable talent like Vincent on a high perch, away from the common folk.

Maynard looked up, ready to rattle off about a dozen questions to Lochlan, who might answer in place of the working necromancer, but noticing his perturbed expression, Maynard paused. He turned back toward the spectacle.

Something was changing. The halo of ghoulish green magic and shadowy skulls billowed out, dispelling into an eerie fog over the immediate area. Vincent lowered to the ground. He turned toward the crew with his mouth hanging wide open like the horn of an old-fashioned record player. From his throat came a dull click, reminiscent of a needle dropping onto vinyl.

Rich grain filtered the sound. "Wh-where am I? What's going on?" From Vince's motionless mouth, a voice entirely unlike his own emerged.

"That's new...." Lochlan installed himself between Vincent and the rest of the crew.

"Am I on the station? Where is everyone?" The voice asked.

Maynard stared, jaw agape. Right before them stood Vincent, possessed. "That's incredible!" He smacked Lochlan's shoulder and approached the spirit with his arm outstretched for a handshake. "Excuse me, I'm Dr. Maynard Percival. Am I speaking with Dr. F'vr?"

The entity swiveled Vincent's head, trying to recall. "Am I? Yes? Yes, of course I am!" Loftily, the doctor brought Vincent's hands to his hips. "What are you all standing around for? Let's get going!" Dr. F'vr moved

Vincent's body like wind in a sheet. He flung himself toward the door of the shattered cockpit.

"Hey, wait a sec!" Lochlan lunged, but failed to grab Vincent's suit.

"I did it. I can't believe I actually did it!" Dr. F'vr mused as he slammed the button to open the door. It was as if he had not even noticed the state of the cabin, blown to pieces and half gone. Clearly, the artificial gravity had been disconnected, yet the doctor confidently leapt at the missing pilot's seat and sent Vincent's body hurtling into space.

"Oh, no you don't!" Without a moment's hesitation, Lochlan charged forward, slapped a tether around a pipe on the wall and jumped out of the cockpit. He lunged for his husband's body and—thankfully—grasped Vincent's suit before it was too late.

The pipe cracked under Lochlan's weight and water burst from it. The spill froze on contact with the negative temperatures of open space, rapidly transforming the room into a cage of ice. "Shit! Lochlan, get back here!" Maynard yelled. Lochlan hooked the other end of the tether onto Vincent's suit. Havoc and Maynard yanked them to safety.

"What are you doing?!" Dr. F'vr kicked and swung around angrily, trying to escape Lochlan's hold. "I have to bring it down! I have to bring it back to the lab!"

Maynard assisted Lochlan in forcing the doctor back into the main area and shutting off access to the cockpit.

"Well, I hope you didn't leave anything important in there," Havoc said. Ice overtook the window. The cockpit was officially off limits.

Though losing patience, Lochlan handled Vincent's body with care. He placed Dr. F'vr down, the tether still affixed to him like a dog on a leash. "Listen doc, you're just a little confused right now...."

Dr. F'vr pushed Lochlan away. "Get off me! I have half a mind to shoot you!"

Lochlan licked his teeth. "I'd sure like to see you try."

Maynard wedged himself between them. "Please, Dr. F'vr. Why don't we take a seat, then we can figure things out together." He placed a hand on Vincent's shoulder.

The hand was thrown back at him. "Just who the hell are you? Who allowed you on my station?!"

Maynard failed to draw up a convincing response before he was shoved aside. Prepared to scold Havoc, he bit his tongue, noticing that they had assumed the disguise of one researcher from the photograph. The woman with a slick bun and narrow glasses was the head of the medical team.

"Dr. F'vr." Havoc replicated the feminine human voice they'd heard from the security footage.

Dr. F'vr looked at Havoc and grabbed his head. "Oh...oh. Dr. Harris. It's you. Where did you...?"

"Good day, Dr. F'vr! These gentlemen are here to fix the pilot controls. They are not working...so good. Remember?"

"The controls aren't working?" Dr. F'vr looked at the cockpit and tilted his head. The door remained iced shut despite his repeated attempts to get in.

"That's right. I understand you want to take the station down but the controls are as good as an umbrella in a tsunami. We'll head straight down. Later."

"Oh...right... Well, hurry the hell up! We need to bring this thing back down to the lab."

Havoc squinted. "Riiight. The lab. And we're bringing...what again? I forget."

Dr. F'vr huffed. "I can't believe they let an ignoramus like you be a doctor." He reached for his forehead. The helmet startled him. He attempted twice more to touch his head before giving up. "When we get back, I'm reporting every single one of you for your incompetence!"

Maynard knew that volatile look on Havoc's face well. "And who exactly are you reporting me to? I'm sorry I'm such an *incompetent ignoramus* that it slipped my mind...fucking prick." Havoc groused the insult under their breath.

"For God's sake, Dr. Harris. You do *work* for Echelon, don't you?"

"Son of a bitch," Maynard exhaled, his blood broiling beneath his skin. He should have suspected the company's avaricious, grimy claws would have sunk into something like this.

Havoc plastered on a fake smile. "Oh, I had a feeling you were going to say that."

Maynard's leaving Echelon had–unfortunately–not been the last time he'd had to deal with them. While they'd lost a great deal of public support, they now operated in the shadows, peddling their fatuous tech in the slimiest, darkest corners in the galaxy, too often turning Leviathan's Luck into a cleaning crew.

Dr. F'vr looked out into some imaginary place beyond the ceiling. "Once they see what we've accomplished here, I'm going to be the richest man in the galaxy!"

"Sure. That's how that works," Havoc said flatly.

"Dr. Harris, you should be grateful to be paired up with someone like me! And you'll all be lucky to have your name on this project despite not having done a damn thing. They said it couldn't be done, but *I* did it! Time travel, the real deal."

"Son of a bitch!" Maynard blurted. Everyone gawked at him, but stares be damned. He would lunge out and choke the man in front of him if it were not for the fact that he was already dead.

He felt a tug on his shoulder. "Hey, this is coming from me: you need to keep cool," Lochlan whispered.

"Can you believe this!?" Maynard huffed. "Time travel research is forbidden for a reason!"

"I hear you, but the ghost is all agitated. Let's not piss it off while it's in my husband's body."

Lochlan was right. Maynard had promised safety would be the priority and the crew couldn't afford to squander this opportunity for intel, no matter how satisfying it would be to eject this lunatic into space.

Maynard straightened his back. "Sir, we'll be starting on those repairs now."

"About damn time! I'm heading to the operating room, Dr. Harris. Join me."

Maynard's compromised heart found the power to leap into this throat; his most important promise was that the creature would be secure within the operating room. Everyone shouting at him pulled Dr. F'vr back.

"No! The operating room is...also...in need of repairs?" Havoc said.

"What? Just what the hell is going on around here?"

"Sorry, doc. It's the whole station. Electrical problems." Lochlan said, reliable as ever in course correcting.

"Yes, why don't you take a seat and tell these fine gentlemen about your research?" Havoc pushed the doctor to take a seat on a built-in bench. "Lord knows you academic types just love to drone on—"

Lochlan smacked the back of Havoc's helmet and flashed a toothy smile. "Yeah, I've always wanted to know a famous person before they got famous!"

"Please, go ahead."

"I don't know...." The doctor scratched the helmet as if he were scratching his chin. "Well, since I'm about to turn in my thesis, anyway." He leaned against the wall. "Our so-called 'team' officially started trials about a year ago but this has been a project of mine for decades. Until now, the only thing holding me back was funding."

"I wonder why?" Maynard rolled his eyes.

"Ah, damn regulations set up by a bunch of cowards but, this group, Echelon, well, they're not afraid to do what needs to be done. For the common good, naturally."

Unable to mask his expression, Maynard had to turn fully around and pretend to work on the cockpit. He tested if the spirit would be too disoriented to notice he wasn't doing anything more than patting the walls randomly. "How did you come across this group?"

"They approached me! They understood the work I was doing and my vision for a brighter future!" It seems Dr. F'vr did not notice, too busy patting himself on the back. "And we're giving the gift to a select group of individuals. Awfully charitable, but I needed to test it somehow."

Maynard turned around. "A gift? Test how?"

"Aren't you paying attention? The *gift* of time travel! It's no wonder you're just a repairman." Dr. F'vr folded his arms. Maynard glanced over at Havoc, desiring some semblance of tranquility to wash over him at the sight of his beloved partner. Instead, he snorted, realizing that

Havoc and Lochlan were miming beating up the doctor. They snapped back into their characters when he turned to look at them. "People like you can't understand. This is important work! What I've done here is going to change the trajectory of sentientkind for the better."

Though decades passed, the dreadful tasks Echelon gave Maynard were fresh in his memory. Beneath a promise to 'save' the planet hid corrupt politically motivated funding, environmentally damaging technology development, and exploitative labor practices. 'Save the planet'. What a load of horseshit. The Echelon Group was as unprincipled as they were parasitic, elevated by the work of others actually trying to do good while they sought to burn a hole in the Earth for profit.

Maynard once thought of himself as a champion of science. By the time he realized he was simply a rabbit leading wolves to the den, it was too late.

He clicked his teeth. "*Right*. Considering you're such a 'charitable' man doing this for the sake of 'sentientkind.' I'm sure you've already considered the consequences. Really, what threat is The Butterfly Effect? Temporal paradoxes must be an easier clean up than they sound! What *possible* motivation could a person in a position of power have to abuse a system like this?"

The doctor sat up and tilted his head at the crew. "Wait a minute...you're not a repairman at all, are you?"

Finally, Maynard thought as he dropped the act. "No! Like I have been trying to tell you I am Dr. Percival and I am here—"

Dr. F'vr leapt from his seat. "You're here to steal my research!"

"What? Of course not!" Given the choice, Maynard would sooner endure a thousand grocery stores than engage with Echelon ever again.

"Well, you can't have it! It's mine, damn it!" Dr. F'vr backed away as the crew circled him.

"Relax. Nobody wants your research," Lochlan gruffed.

"Can we be done with this cretin?" Havoc asked. Lochlan pushed them. "I mean, Dr. F'vr your research is safe. Just calm down."

"No! No, you're lying!" Disorientation swayed the doctor back and forth.

When Lochlan reached for the spirit to steady him, Dr. F'vr dove around Havoc and then around Maynard. Repeatedly, Lochlan tried to grab hold of Vincent's body, but he would not sit still.

Maynard felt a sudden tug at his waist, pulled forward into Havoc. Before Maynard could react, the rope from the tether wrapped his arms to his sides. "Wait, Lochlan! Stop moving!"

Suddenly, the three crewmates found themselves coiled together like a nest of snakes. Dr. F'vr, leading the jumble, pulled as hard as he could to run away, but an unexpected game of tug-o-war ensued. The crew leaned back together. In a state of panic, the doctor struggled with the fastener at his side. He swatted at the clasp like an insect. By a lucky strike, he knocked the clasp off and freed himself. The crew tumbled backward, falling into a pile. By the time Maynard looked up, the doctor was already gone.

Squashed by the two larger men, Havoc heaved, "Fantastic display of idiocy, boys. A round of applause for the Tweedle brothers!"

Lochlan kneed Havoc in the rib. "Will you shut up and give me some room?"

With the doctor gone, Havoc could end the charade. They shifted into a smaller version of themself. Their deflated suit allowed Lochlan the room he needed to deploy the knife function of his arm. The small blade extended from his wrist and he hurried to cut them out.

The crew stood up to crane their stiff backs, flinching when a shrill screech carried from down another chamber. An ominous roar preceded the sounds of Dr. F'vr shouting and two sets of feet rapidly approaching.

Lochlan hammered out the word "Fuck!" about a dozen times as he bolted for the center in a panic, followed closely by Maynard and Havoc.

Maynard threw his head around the corner to find the makings of a worse case scenario. In the west wing was

Vincent's body, running toward the center at full speed, pursued by the creature.

Long-Distance
Chapter 19

//Vince

As Vince floated on his back in the shallows of an oasis, tiny, shimmering fish brushed against him. Guarded by ghostly desert animals, rocked by cool water, and lulled by the rushing of a nearby waterfall, he could have kept sleeping until the end of time. Or until he was forced awake by Dr. F'vr's shouting.

Vince's eyes flew open. He remembered where he was. The doctor had just knocked him over and Vince sat up, swinging at something that wasn't there. "Back up, asshole!"

The dream left him disoriented. Where Dr. F'vr had been moments ago, was now Lochlan. The two were on the ground, Vince on top of his husband, and he felt soreness in his leg, as if someone had yanked on it. He kicked his leg up to see what was weighing it down. Havoc had a tentacle wrapped tightly around the ankle.

They reeled the tentacle into their suit to put their glove back on. "Your delicate flower is heavier than he looks."

Lochlan sat up, rubbing his back. "Ugh. Did you have to throw him at me?"

"What are those muscles for, anyway? I'll be more considerate the next time I'm saving lives."

"What?" Vince patted himself down for reassurance that he was back in his own body. "You saved me? From what? What happened?"

He understood the basics; the doctor had snatched his body. With nowhere to go, Vince's spirit remained asleep in the Veil while Dr. F'vr could do whatever he wanted. Vince's absence left him in the dark, but he was relieved to find he hadn't traveled far. The crew was still near the cockpit.

"Ah, you're home," Havoc said through tight lips.

In search of a proper answer, Vince's dazed gaze swept across the disgruntled crew, each person positioned in a separate corner of the station's smallest chamber. He wanted to ask again what happened, but a loud slam and earsplitting shriek from the other side of the door startled him. He kicked away from the door and clung to his husband.

"Keep your voices down!" Maynard's whisper came out in a sizzle as he removed his finger from the door's lockpad to shush them. That door was open before. It was probably a good thing that it was closed now.

"What the hell was that?" Vince asked. Hopefully, that wasn't the sound he thought it was.

Havoc stood over Vince with his arms folded. "That's your question to answer. While you were away, your substitute hosted a show and tell."

Vince's heart dropped into his lap. "The doctor? You're kidding." He was almost certain they were not. Dr. F'vr—and by extension Vince—must have caused this. Whatever this was. "Please be kidding?" Silence. "Will someone tell me what's going on?"

"Right now we're trapped between the creature you set loose on us and a wall of ice." Havoc threw out their arms, gesturing at the only two exits to the chamber. Vince saw the small window to the cockpit completely frozen over. What had he done? Havoc turned to address the crew. "Now that Vince has arrived, shall we discuss who will eat whom first? I have preferences for the order."

A pat on the back reminded Vince that he was still resting on his poor, aching husband. "You could have given us a heads up before you let that guy run around. He nearly got you killed," Lochlan said, tone curbed. Even with the helmet on, Vince could see Lochlan's face turning red up to the tips of his ears.

He felt a shameful knot form in his throat, difficult to talk over. "Normally, they let me get a word in! I've never had someone just steal a ride like that." He stood, dusted himself off, and extended a hand to help Lochlan up. "*Pinche culero.* He can find his own way to the city."

"He'll figure it out." Lochlan stood, then groaned into a stretch. Vince automatically shifted into caretaker mode, focusing on massaging the sore muscle, but the bulky suit prevented much sensation. Lochlan patted Vince's hands to stop him. Vince took a step back, guilt settling on his cheeks. He was completely useless.

"Yeah, they can be like that," Maynard dismissed, tapping away at his log again. "Just a quick round of questions." He approached Vince, comm held out to record the answers. "What do you see when you enter the Veil? When a spirit possesses you, are you not able to regain control of your body? Do spirits have a sense of taste and smell?"

"Can we talk about this later?" Vince squeaked, feeling like he'd entered a press-conference naked.

Maynard looked around at the crew awkwardly before he muttered, "Well, you never know what might be useful information." He brushed off the embittered looks and spoke into his comm, "What time is it?"

The computer's voice came through. "Leviathan's Luck's computer is reading April 18th, 0244 hours."

All the air pushed out of Vince's lungs. "It's been a *week?*"

Havoc kicked the wall and threw their arms in the air. Maynard screwed his face tight. He peered at them out of the corner of his eye. Before Vince could ask what that was all about, Havoc shouldered him aside to close in on Lochlan. "Did you have to tether yourself to a *water pipe*, of all things?"

Lochlan's chest pushed back against Havoc, and the force caused them to stumble. "How was I supposed to know? I didn't see you coming up with anything."

"Oh, we would have gotten Vince back eventually! I knew you were going to be too precious about him."

"What happened to 'Vince is our top priority'?"

"Technically, I promised you that 'safety' would be our top priority," Maynard said.

Havoc's mouth stretched to a thin line. "Well, I can't imagine anything safer than flinging yourself into space." Vince almost didn't want to know what they were talking about. He was too afraid to cut into the argument anyway.

Lochlan folded his arms. "Oh, so this is my fault?"

"Well, partially," Maynard answered.

"*Entirely*," Havoc revised.

"If you two hadn't tipped the doctor off, we would be fine right now!"

"Excuse you! My performance was flawless." Havoc punctuated with a sarcastic curtsy.

Lochlan confronted the bow with a skeptical click of his teeth. "Yeah, real convincing. You sound just like a scientist. Insulting the guy and 'forgetting' the name of the place you work for. You lie all damn day and that's the best you could do?"

Havoc brought a hand to their chest and scoffed. "*Maynard* is the one who couldn't keep in character! What kind of repairman gives a shit about 'temporal paradoxes'?!" Regardless of whether Vince understood what 'temperature pretax' meant, he couldn't follow any of this. He must have been out for a while.

Lochlan turned his focus to Maynard now. "You couldn't have waited to give the guy the third degree?"

Feigning indifference, Maynard shook his head and turned away from his companions to his comm. "Well, my apologies for not coddling the son of a bitch. Next time we meet a serial killer, I'll treat them to coffee."

Lochlan looked up at the ceiling. "You *always* have to be right about everything."

"I don't *have* to be, I just am. And currently, I am right about the fact that we are where we are because *you* never think before acting and *you* never take anything seriously." With a strict finger, he pointed at Lochlan and then Havoc respectively.

"*No*. We wouldn't be in *this* particular situation if Lochlan's husband could keep his own skin on," Havoc thumped Lochlan's arm.

With the spotlight now on his own failings, Vince shrunk into his suit, wishing to disappear. He was supposed to be a master of his craft, but he made such a stupid mistake. How–*how*–could he let himself become possessed?

It was like he time traveled back to the moment he decided to leave the church and magic for good. Stained glass shattered on the ground. Smoke billowed from every window. The whole city gathered before the cathedral, murmuring around him, "Father Luque?", "What's happening?", "What did he do?"

Whether it was the nature of necromancy or his own personal failings, he just couldn't seem to use his magic without hurting others. It took three decades to shut that window, but the second it opened he jumped right through. What a totally selfish move. And he convinced himself it was a sign.

It was a test.

Lochlan's lip curled into a forced grin, too stunned to react appropriately. "*Fuck* you. You were the ones who strong-armed him into coming along!"

Maynard folded his arms. "Nobody forced him to do anything."

"Vince wouldn't even be here at all if you could think with your other head," Havoc taunted.

The low blow set Lochlan off, red and rigid like a brick. "That's it! I'm kicking your ass!"

Without thinking, Vince jumped into the center of the yelling men, protecting them from each other. "Stop it!

Everyone just stop! Why are you mad at each other? This is my fault!" Confused, the crew backed away from him.

Lochlan closed his eyes and released an exasperated sigh through his nostrils. Constantly undermining himself, for Vince's sake, must be exhausting. "Vinni, it's not your fault."

Vince refused to accept that. For everything that happened—everything—he could only blame himself. It was his insistence to move in, his demand to come along on the mission, and his spell that stuck the crew literally between a rock and a hard place.

"Yes, it is. I forced you to bring me and now look at us. *All* of you were right." If only he had listened sooner. "I shouldn't be here."

Maynard and Havoc fell silent, exchanging stiff glances before withdrawing to a far corner. It would be hopeless to give the other couple the real privacy they needed, but they did their best and turned away.

With unusual fragility, Lochlan guided them toward the opposite corner. "What are you saying?"

Vince couldn't bring himself to look at Lochlan, kneading the leg of his suit anxiously to soothe the wild magic pooling in his fingertips. He knew what he *should* say, but the words were like any other spell. Once he said it, it would be real, and then he'd have to do it. But Gods, he really, really, *really* didn't want to. "I think...when we leave...." He avoided using 'if'–discussing the odds of that wouldn't help anyone right now. "Maybe I should go back to Earth for a bit." There. It was out.

"What? Hey, let's not do anything rash." Lochlan sounded so small. Smaller than Vince had ever heard.

"Lochlan, this *whole thing* was rash. Since we got married, all I've done is make your life harder; your home, your work, your relationship with your friends...." Hesitantly, Vince met his husband's eye. Huge mistake.

A heavy gray brow settled over Lochlan's dejected eyes like fog over a forest. "That's not true."

Vince forced out a weak smile to comfort them both. "You don't have to lie. I don't want to ruin what we have by rushing it. A little space might be good for us."

Lochlan attempted a smile in return, but it came out wavering and miserable. "Vince, you're breaking my heart here," he cracked through an insincere chuckle. Vince tried to push back the sinking feeling that Lochlan really meant that.

To control the surging magic in his chest, Vince grasped his husband's hands, breathing deeply and counting to four. "Lochlan, please try to understand."

Lochlan straightened his back and fixed his attention on the ground. "No, yeah...I get it." The helmet blocked his expression. Vince wasn't sure if he imagined the sniffle between words.

He needed to stay strong, trusting that their flame couldn't be dimmed by any time apart. Lochlan didn't know it right now but this could make his life so much better and Vince would do anything for his husband's happiness.

"I just think if we give it a few months, we'll be better prepared for the real thing." Vince said. "A little time and we'll be in a different place."

"A different place...." Maynard's whispered remark came out of nowhere. Vince had forgotten about the other couple. Havoc stepped on Maynard's foot. "I-I'm sorry. I'm not listening. Forget I'm here."

Lochlan addressed the floor. "I'll get us out of here. We'll work the rest out later." Lochlan walked away and Vince felt the comforting weight of his husband's hand vanish.

GROSSER.

CHAPTER 20

//Havoc

Havoc leaned up against the wall, staring at Maynard's comm. The habitual snooping was unsuccessful. Maynard was only reviewing mission details. If they didn't want to dwell on their failures as a friend and their involvement in Lochlan's relationship crashing and burning, all they could do was hum the chorus of the song from the shuttle that was now stuck in their head.

Lochlan approached with his head hung low. "I know we have to get out of here, but I'm gonna take a second." Havoc picked up on the frailest crack in his voice. Small and sharp, it was like a needle in their chest.

"Sure," Maynard said. Lochlan turned toward a corner and leaned against the wall, facing away from everyone. The couple remained silent for some time, almost daring the other to speak first, and Havoc was not going to lose this one.

Maynard tapped his fingers on the back of his hand. Either he was practicing for the drumline or he was craving a cigarette. "This is our fault," he sighed.

Havoc leaned back, supported by the wall behind them. "No, darling, you misheard. Vince just said it was *his* fault."

"Havoc, enough games. We are hurting Lochlan."

Guilt crept its revolting way up Havoc's stomach lining to carve out a ward in their chest. The entire experience left them feeling ill once again. An overwhelming impulse to scurry away was thwarted only because there was nowhere to run to. They could shift as small as possible and hide in their own boot. That might not go over so well with Maynard.

"He's hurting himself. I don't understand why he doesn't argue. He never lets anyone push him around like this."

Maynard shook his head. "Vincent isn't pushing him around. He's trying to tell Lochlan what they need, and he only feels like they need it because of our actions."

"Not just *our* actions," Havoc debated. Maynard shook his head. Havoc stood no chance against this Maynard, the worst kind of Maynard; not angry, but disappointed. "But, partly. I guess."

"Then?"

"Then...Vince needs to get used to it if they're ever going to make this thing work. The home, the job, the pig-headed way Lochlan can be...us." 'Us,' the most important part in Havoc's opinion. 'Us' was the thing that was going to stick around long after the missions came to an end. Havoc especially so. If Vince were married to Lochlan, he might as well have married the team.

Maynard stared at Havoc. The intensity had them feeling like a butterfly pinned to a board. "Havoc...you really like Vincent, don't you?"

"Ha!" The laugh came out as a knee-jerk reaction. "We had a semi-decent night out together. I was only there to dig into his psyche. Just doing my due diligence as a member of the crew." Havoc tried to stop himself from talking but couldn't, the words running out of him like water from the broken pipe. If only it would crystalize him too. "I can get along with anyone if I'm drunk enough, can't you? I mean, sure, we had a friendly conversation, and maybe I felt a touch of empathy—sympathy! More like pity, really. Other than that, I hardly consider the Father at all. He doesn't like to be called that, you know, 'Father.' But what do I care? So 'Father Luque' he is! In all honesty, I preferred the ghost—"

Maynard lowered his lids and pressed the glass of his helmet to Havoc's with a delicate but rather dazzling smirk. "Darling, please don't hide from me."

Havoc's eyes widened in fear and fondness as their defenses crumbled. "He called me 'your Highness.' No one aside from you has called me that in a very long time."

Maynard smiled. "We should apologize to our new friend," he said. *A new friend.* All at once, Havoc's exceptionally long life seemed slightly more tolerable.

Damn it. Havoc threw Maynard off. They knew he was right, but that would not make degrading themself any easier. "Fine." The deer-eyed choirboy was going to be the death of them.

Maynard tugged Havoc by their suit over to Vince. A dense aurora hung around the teary-eyed spellcaster. Gods, did this man ever stop crying?

"I'm sorry. I know we're in a rush," Vince said, straightening up. He tried to wipe the tears from his face but hit the glass.

Havoc crossed their arms. "Why are these helmets so difficult to remember?"

"Vincent—Vince," Maynard started. "I am not the best at this sort of thing, but you deserve an apology for what's happened here." It was almost inconceivable, Maynard Percival not only using a nickname for a stranger but placing his hand on that stranger's shoulder to comfort him. If anyone in the universe was as bad with people as Havoc, it was him. "I am sure that you are feeling frightened and frustrated, but, *believe me*, precarious situations and explosive arguments are not at all unusual for us."

Skeptically, Vince tilted his head. He was silent for a moment. "Do you mean that?" he asked, stupid hopeful look in his stupid hopeful eyes.

With a light, warm chuckle, Maynard nodded. "We've always spoken to each other like this. Unfortunately. I guess we don't realize just how bizarre that is. You have no reason to think any of this was your fault. We all could have done things differently today, and maybe it would have made a difference. Maybe it wouldn't have. Some of us—all of us—have a hard time admitting that."

Vince sniffled. "Thank you for saying that, Maynard."

"It's the truth. That I am *very* right about." Maynard gestured for Havoc's turn under the spotlight.

Uncomfortably, they took a step forward. "I am 'sorry' for 'being difficult.'" They were nudged.

"Ahem. Excuse him." Maynard walked away, allowing them the privacy to do this the right way.

For a moment, Havoc's brain ceased operating. A showman's grin stretched across their face. "So, we put it to a vote and the majority rules. This is not your fault, and you're not leaving!"

"Very funny." Vince seemed to be somewhere else.

Havoc tightly clasped their hands behind their back to prevent themself from killing Vince just so they didn't have to do this. "Look." This was going to be a fucking nightmare. "You weren't *entirely* wrong the other night." Vince blinked at Havoc with his obnoxiously long, baby-doll lashes. Oh Gods, killing him would be so much easier. "For *some* reason, I find myself rooting for you as a couple. You two are so disgustingly obsessed with each other it gives me hope of finding true love myself one day," Havoc joked, looking back at Maynard, undoubtedly the all the stars in their sky. Vince laughed, so Havoc pressed on, feeling braver. "And *maybe* when it comes to the lubber, I am a bit protective or...."

"Jealous?"

Havoc stomped. "Well, I was here first, you know! You give a man twenty-five of the best years of your life and he leaves you for a younger man! It's disgraceful!" Vince laughed harder, water from his eyes disappearing into a shiny pool of ink. Havoc gave in. Vince had won the war. "So you were right about me, after all. It wouldn't be a terrible idea to have a translator around. Those two can really pile it on, and I need someone here to tip the scales in my favor. Not to mention, it would be beyond selfish of you to leave when you've seen the state of our kitchen. You're a man of the tome. Shouldn't you care more for your neighbor or whatever?"

The surrounding air was so much lighter, Vince spilling with laughter and small stars. It was as nice a sound as Lochlan gloried. "So, if I'm understanding this right, I should stay. Not because of how it would affect my relationship or Lochlan's happiness, and definitely not because you might actually *miss* me, but because if I leave, you'll be outnumbered and everyone will starve to death?"

"Yes, exactly! Finally! Someone around here has a sense of compassion for me!" Havoc looked up to the ceiling in feigned elation. "And while we would *eventually* forgive you for selfishly abandoning such a noble cause...this is a chance to do something 'important.'"

Vince smiled warmly, shaking his head. "Yeah, I don't think Lochlan is ever going to invite me on a mission again."

"Well, it's not up to him. His boss sure has taken a liking to you. You should have seen him all giddy when you pulled out the *Danse Macabre*. The pervert."

Vince tried to throw a hand over his mouth in shock. "Oh my gods, Havoc! You can't say that!"

"Oh, you were gonna figure it out. He is *not* subtle." Havoc grabbed Vince by the shoulders and pushed him in Lochlan's direction. "Now go kiss and make up before your husband murders me."

Vince nodded, took a deep breath, and looked back at Havoc. With a thank you, he headed off.

Maynard stepped back over and pulled Havoc in by their waist. Their bodies pressed together, Havoc hid behind their helmet. In their private channel, Maynard said, "You did good."

Havoc pushed into Maynard with his hip, rocking them both. "Did *well*, my star."

"Oh. I like it when you talk grammar."

Havoc pinched Maynard's side, mocking, "Is *someone* in the mood because he saw a shiny new monstrosity to-day?"

Maynard coughed, his face turning a stunning vermil-lion. "Don't joke like that. It's not funny."

"There's no sense in hiding it. We *all* know."

Maynard swallowed. "A-all?"

"*All.*"

It was Maynard's turn to look for places to hide. "Good lord. I really am never going to look him in the eye again."

Big Feelings

Chapter 21

//Lochlan

Lochlan leaned against the wall, hiding behind his own back. His throat tightened as he struggled to contain something that felt far too large, even for his body.

Right now he'd wish on every star, pluck every four-leaf clover, and hang a horseshoe on every wall if it meant this wouldn't be the beginning of the end. Sadly, he was no stranger to this. He knew the signs. Vince was always too good for him. It was only a matter of time before he caught on.

"Loch?" Vince's voice came from behind him, sweet but cautious. Lochlan felt a hand on his back and the sting of salt in his eye. Instinctively, his fist balled as if it might intimidate his own tears from coming out. He couldn't look at Vince. It might just break the dam.

"Oh, hey there, sweetheart."

"Lochlan, look at me," Vince said. Everything in Lochlan's history told him to push away, but—given any invitation from his husband—he would always come running. He faced Vince, eyes red and wet. Vince clutched his chest. "Oh, Gods... I am *such* an idiot. How could I think I would ever leave you?"

"What? Really?"

"Yes, really. I am so sorry. I am all over the place right now." Vince rubbed soothing circles on Lochlan's chest. Even though he could hardly feel it through the suit, the touch was just like medicine. "I'm just scared."

Lochlan wrapped his arms around his husband. "We're gonna get out of here." He had no doubts about that.

"No." Vince exhaled, a breath he seemed to have held for ages. "I'm scared of *you*. We did this really crazy thing and I think it was the best decision I've ever made but I am so worried you're going to wake up one day and think you made a huge mistake. All we've done these last few days is fight and if I'm already causing you this much trouble, think about all the damage I could do in a month or in a year...."

"I fight everybody. I'm working on it, but I swear I'm getting better."

Vince smiled faintly. "So I've been told."

Lochlan's whole body ached to be closer. He rested his helmet against Vince's and confessed, "For what it's worth, you scare the hell out of me."

Vince took Lochlan's hands and squeezed them with a light swing. "Okay. So we're both scared. The best way to get through that is together. Right?"

"You know, you're really giving me whiplash." A tender laugh passed between them. "I just want to kiss you right now."

"I know, right?" Vince hummed. "I love you."

"I love you too."

Lochlan pulled Vince into a hug so tight it could have welded them together. The suits, the station, and the banging on the other side of the door faded away. For a moment, it was just the two of them. When Lochlan resurfaced from that peaceful place, he found a new motivation to get the hell out of here. He puffed out his chest, stretched his neck, and approached the crew. Nothing was going to stand in the way of that kiss.

Maynard's fingers were flying over the keyboard. Hearing Lochlan's footsteps, he looked up from his comm to ask, "Good?"

Lochlan replied with a firm, "Good."

"Good!" Havoc chimed.

Maynard folded his arms behind his back and bounced on his heel. "Now that that's over, I have a lot to say."

Havoc slid over to stand between the other two, their scrunched mouth an apology for the bluntness. "Of course you do."

Lochlan could forgive it. It took a lot for Maynard to sit on something when he felt it was important enough.

All attention was on the captain as he paced the wall like a duck in a carnival shooting game. "Let me start by expressing that this entire situation has been *bewildering*, to say the least. I mean, time travel? Pfft, really? Ridiculous as it seemed, it *was* a convenient explanation for a lot of what's happened: the selective density of the asteroid field, the delay in communications, 'jumping forward' in time. *That's* what made me think. Since entering a certain range of the station, we haven't been moving through time sporadically—forward and backwards—time has only moved forward. Why is that?" Nobody answered, it was pointless. "I had my doubts, but I needed more information, and I learned one valuable piece of intel from talking to the doctor myself." Everyone stared at the captain, impatiently waiting for the grand reveal. "The man is an idiot. So, Percival, cast aside what you've been told and what do you see?" Apparently, he boarded solo on his train of thought. "An unregistered station acting as an operating room, a quantum tunneling device logged as 'medical supplies', and a missing patient in distress. All collected by an abusive, money-hungry, incompetent—"

"*Pierce.*"

"—bastard with no morals and no respect for real medical practice," he blurted it like one big word. "I know, I know! Back to the point—"

"With haste, dear." Havoc moved their hand in circles.

"Guys, shh!" Vince elbowed Lochlan and Havoc. The captain's notorious logic-vomit was still a novelty to Vince. His enthusiasm was cute, in a way. Maynard seemed to agree, thanking Vince while Lochlan's attention drifted off. *I could probably eat my way out of the ice.*

Lochlan came back down when Maynard spoke to him directly. "A quantum tunneling device can create *wormholes*. With all of that in mind...." Maynard handed over Xijax's journal from their first trip and opened it to a bookmark towards the end. "What does that look like to you, pilot?"

Lochlan stared at the journal's last pages. He saw this last time; the spiraled drawings. Nothing came to mind. It was only when Maynard took his thumb to the edge and flipped through the pages like a flip-book cartoon that Lochlan recognized it. Space. Ripples like a tunnel and shifting colors. Then space again. Exactly how it would look from the pilot's seat.

Lochlan's eyes widened. "Oh shit! It looks like a wormhole!" Ignoring the warnings of fellow spacers, the crew hopped through wormholes to escape a sticky situation. He flipped through the pages again. The bright colors, the stars, the spirals to show something moving fast and turbulent. It was like he was traveling through it now. "Damn, I feel bad for talking shit earlier. This is pretty decent."

Vince whistled to get the crew's attention. "Hello? Professional space cowboys? I'm here too." Lochlan held out the notebook to Vince like it would offer any sort of clarification. "*Nada.*"

"To put this simply—you're familiar with wormholes, right?" Maynard posed the question like he was asking about a good friend of theirs.

Vince glanced around, making sure the question was for him. "No?"

"Okay!" A lottery winner couldn't have grinned wider than Maynard. He probably would have held Vince for hours if they had time. He projected a diagram of a c-shaped plane and a vertical tunnel between the ends from his comm and spun it around. "A wormhole is a topological feature of spacetime. Essentially, it is a structure that acts as a passageway between two distant points in the universe. With each end of the tunnel at different points in spacetime, it allows for faster travel than what conventional, linear travel would permit." Only *the* Dr. Percival could trigger that kind of deeply confused look. "Er, it's like a shortcut? Similar to your tattoo, Vince." Vince looked at his chest and over his shoulder with a wrinkled nose. "The nature of the one we ran into was the root of the time anomaly, but not in how we or the doctor believed. Theoretically, if the two ends of a wormhole are close enough, then the surrounding space would be drawn to multiple points at once. If so, a group of unlucky passersby might find themselves stalled between both points. From an outside perspective, we're not jumping through time. We're simply holding still for long periods."

Vince's eyes lit up. He may have actually followed this better than anyone else. "The doctor told me the asteroid 'wasn't there and then it was.' When he crashed into it, he couldn't see it coming but it's not like it came out of nowhere. While they were holding still, it was still moving!"

"Yes! Exactly, Vincent!" Maynard clapped.

"Wait." Vince grimaced, looking as sick as he did back in the shuttle. "Does that mean it could happen again?"

"Yes!" Excitement took over Maynard's tact. "But, uhm. Try not to think about that. So now that we've confirmed that there is a wormhole on board, would anyone like to guess where it is?" He looked about ready to explode.

Lochlan was over the long-winded explanation. Folding his arms, he caught the glint of his cybernetic arm—nothing but a pile of scrap just days ago—and a realization struck him. "Fuck me. It's the thing!"

"The thing?" Vince's jaw dropped. "You stuck your arm into a *wormhole*?"

"And lived! Take that science! I'm never gonna die!" Carried away by the excitement of discovery with Maynard, Lochlan threw up his arms and they high-fived. Six decades and tough enough to punch a wormhole? As far as he was concerned, he was the strongest man in the universe. Havoc rained on the parade, smacking the back of their helmets.

"Don't be so sure of that," Vince threatened. "So, if we're saying the researchers use that device to make wormholes and we know they're doing shady surgeries then...." He rubbed his stomach. His face twisted into something sour. "I'm just thinking that...with all that anger I've been feeling around this place–I mean, if I had to guess, that pissed off spirit I've been seeing is probably the patient?"

Maynard nodded like he hated to agree. "I'm afraid we have an official name for the creature."

Havoc sighed heavily. "Xijax." They looked out at the crew in a rare, sobering scene. Nobody spoke. A moment of silence passed for Xijax.

Lochlan chewed his lip. "Vinni, there's not anything we can do for him, is there?"

Vince shook his head. "He belongs to the Veil. If it's like Maynard said—if he's being stalled—then he's not staying inside long enough to make it to the city, so I think the best thing we can do for him is help him find his way."

"So it's decided. How do we go about killing Xijax?" Havoc asked.

Vince cringed. "Oh, that's not...can we just call it 'laying him to rest'?"

"We need to close the wormhole," Maynard said. "That should release him and resolve the danger. My first thought is to use the quantum tunneling device to destabilize it, but—aside from needing a great deal of power—the collapse would cause an explosion."

Lochlan rubbed his shoulder. "Well, we've got the shuttle. We could use the battery to charge up the shot and if we're all in before it goes off, is that fast enough?"

"That should work well to escape, but we need a *lot* of energy. More than the shuttle could provide."

Lochlan hated what he was about to say, but it looked like their best and only shot. "Well...I think I know a guy." He turned to Vince.

"Oh!" Vince bounced. "I can definitely do that!"

Maynard's grin was unsettling; he was way too pumped about their jerry-rigged plan but if he were feeling confident Lochlan wouldn't argue.

Rubbing his hands together, Maynard said, "Alright, now we just need some room to work. Darling?"

Havoc gave him a lazy salute. "Aye, aye."

"Alright, then!" Maynard stood by the keypad. "Everyone is clear? Havoc will distract Xijax. Lochlan will prepare the shuttle. Vince, you stay with me and we will head for the device." The new crew looked at each other and nodded. "Is everyone ready?"

"Ready."

"On my mark."

Exit Stage Right
Chapter 22

//Vince

Vince whispered a protection prayer for the crew. Clinging to the wall, he stood between Maynard and Lochlan, readied like a stage crew in the wings. All eyes turned to Havoc as he warmed up in the opposite corner, preparing for what they hoped would be a death-defying performance. Havoc gave their onlookers a small, disinterested bow.

From his chest, Maynard counted them down, "Three...two...one!" and slammed the keypad. Like a curtain, the door parted.

From within Havoc's helmet came a glow, and when the light settled, they'd taken on the form of Dr. F'vr, jumping around and banging on the walls for attention. "Hey Xijax!" Havoc bellowed. "You suck!" In a fit of rage, Xijax charged toward Havoc.

"Ha, I get it," Lochlan said.

"Be nice to him!"

Maynard yanked Vince by his sleeve. "Move!" He tore his eyes away from his partner and sprinted for the center. Vince whimpered as he stumbled after the captain.

Lochlan's herculean build and long stride would have made running ahead of them effortless, but—ever the loyal guard—he remained behind, acting as a shield against any unscripted actions from Xijax.

Havoc's jeers echoed as the crew reached the center. Maynard and Vince continued on course toward the supply room. Lochlan sent them ahead, stopping for the ladder that would bring him to the docking bay outside the station. Without hesitation, he scaled the ladder. They were on their own now. Maynard put a protective arm around Vince. Even through the thick fabric, Vince could tell the captain was surprisingly jacked.

Lochlan's rendered voice came through the crew's open communications channel. "Hey, hey. Pim, what's the matter? ...Oh, come on... You've gotta be fucking kidding me!"

"What's wrong?" Maynard asked.

"The shuttle won't turn on. I don't know—" Vince envisioned the tooth-cracking clench of Lochlan's jaw as he growled, "*Hawk.*"

Oops.

"Oops," Havoc piped, amid their dance with Xijax. "Well, I told you I crashed it!"

"I thought you were just saying that to make me feel better!"

Havoc interrupted their sidestepping to put their hands on their hips. "Do you hear yourself when you talk?" When Xijax's arm came down on them, they regained focus and slipped out of its way.

"Both of you, shut up!" The famous vein on Maynard's forehead was on full display. He and Vince had reached the device and needed to focus. Maynard got out his scanner and pressed into a small covering. It popped open to reveal a collection of cable connectors. He began experimenting with commands. Even amidst the chaos, he remained laser-focused. "Lochlan, find us a new way out."

"God damn it. Alright, I think I got something." There were the sounds of rustling and a loud metallic unclasping. "God, if you're out there...you owe me, asshole."

"Watch your mouth," Vince said.

Lochlan made a strained grunt with effort, as if he were pushing something heavy. Moments later, he descended the ladder once more and jogged past Vince toward the end chamber.

Vince's head swiveled to follow. "Where are you—?"

Lochlan threw an arm up to pause the conversation, shouted, "Escape pod," and continued barreling down the hall.

"Vincent, focus." Maynard's scanner emitted a rhythmic beep, seeking a stable connection.

"On it!" Vince placed both his hands on the machine, closed his eyes, and tried to steady his breathing. He attempted to summon a cask of energy from the well of his magic. Glittering emerald energy circled the device. He peeked to see the captain's eyes and smile stretched with the relief that their plan was working.

The celebration may have come too soon. A blood-curdling shriek from down the hall broke Vince's concentration and, with it, his spell. "Shit." He shook his fingers. His eyes remained shut tight as he rubbed his palms together and whispered, "Okay, Vihito, you got this," before trying again. Down the wing, the sound of something striking the escape pod's surface echoed loudly. Vince flinched, and the machine powered down again. "Damn it."

With each attempt, Maynard refreshed his scanner, encouraging it to find the connection. "I need more than this."

"I know! I'm sorry. All that time Dr. F'vr spent in my body really drained my magic, and I'm having trouble concentrating. I just need to, like, get in the zone." Vince shut his eyes again and tried to think of something soothing. Waterfalls in the Veil, Lochlan in the morning, Lochlan in the Veil. *Fuck. Not that.* It was too late. Vince's mind took over, trapping him in a cycle of imagining every worst-case scenario. He envisioned the crew in a row of caskets and froze.

Maynard checked all around them. He was probably hoping a solution would just appear out of thin air. He broke the long, panicked silence by tapping his comm and clearing his throat. "Vince, would you be interested in knowing Lochlan's number of sexual partners?" Vince wrinkled his nose. He'd never given it a thought, although he knew it was a lot, but where the hell was this coming from? Of all times. Maynard ignored the unfavorable look and continued. "Guess a number between zero and five-hundred."

Shock contorted Vince's face. "A-are you serious?" Though his love for Lochlan would endure unchanged, his body shook, as if possessed by the ghost of lovers past.

Maynard, too pleased with himself, hid a smirk. "For nearly two weeks, me and Havoc called you 'Victor' because, well, we thought that was your name and Lochlan never corrected us."

"Lochlan, he better be joking!" Vince took the silence as an even greater insult. His cheeks ran hot. Was this some kind of weird punishment for his failures? He asked himself if Maynard really hated him.

Maynard snapped and pointed at Vince, recalling another horrifying gem. "Those fancy soaps you were looking for after the first night you stayed over? Lochlan bit into it, realized it wasn't chocolate and threw it in the trash." His tight lip and nod signaled Vince was right to be angry.

The summoning of furious embers enveloped Vince. "Oh. My. Gods. I am going to *kill* him!" With inflamed fists, Vince pounded on the machine. "Do you know how expensive those were, you rich jerk?!"

"Yes!" Maynard beamed at his scanner. A high-pitched whirl was now apparent to Vince. In his frustration, he'd completely missed how the energy from his wild magic had powered the machine. A chime from the scanner signaled a successful connection.

Everyone could complain all they wanted, Maynard *was* a genius. His job couldn't have been an easy one–always having to be the one making the hard decisions. Vince knew all too well how impossible it was to keep everyone happy, but Maynard knew when it was better not to. Vince regretted ever doubting him.

With a new found respect for the captain, he finally allowed himself the courtesy of a full-blown meltdown. "Okay, that's it!" He punched the machine again. "I can't believe I have to spend my final moments with *you*, on this *freezing* station, in this ugly-ass outfit!"

"H-hey, I think the design is very flattering."

Continuing to wail on the machine, Vince's soft punches did nothing to the shell, but it felt good to hit something. He was tired, hungry, a little horny, and gods damn it, he was pissed. With each hit, the power crept.

"I look like *The Thing*! I have helmet hair! And I am definitely breaking out! I have never looked more hideous than I do in this! Moment! And that's how I'm going to die!" Vince's last strike energized the machine.

Maynard made quick work of enabling the commands. "Speaking of grave looks," he started. "Here's a fun fact: If you were exposed to the vacuum of space, it would cause the fluids in your skin to vaporize. Bubbles would form in your blood and you would swell to the point of being completely unrecognizable."

Vince blanched, his stomach turning like a waterwheel to sustain the machine's power. "T-that's disgusting. Wait. If that happened, I couldn't have an open casket funeral! That's been in my dream funeral binder since I was a kid!"

Maynard shrugged. "The only thing keeping you from exploding would be your skin and circulatory system. An open casket is out of the question unless you want people to see you bloated like a balloon in a fishnet."

"That's like, my worst nightmare!"

Maynard checked his scanner. After chewing on his cheek, he hummed, "Yeah...." and yanked on Vince's helmet.

"Maynard, stop that!" Vince reeled back, kicking wildly. "What the hell is your problem?!" Magic flew out of Vince in every direction.

Maynard wove between the blasts and kept his grip tight, saying, "Hold still, I'm just trying to take your helmet off."

"Leave me alone!" Vince caught Maynard's wrist and accidentally pressed on his comm.

Lochlan's voice came over the comm. "Hey. Am I back on? Kick his ass, baby!"

"Watch it! You're next in line!" Vince grabbed Maynard's wrists and kicked him in the shin. Maynard curled into himself and Vince threw his hands over his helmet. "Oh my gods! I'm so sorry, Maynard! Are you okay?"

"You have good reflexes." Maynard winced.

"Oh, I took a self-defense class at the—"

"Sounds like you're all having a blast, but when you can, I need an ETA from everyone not staring down Satan's garbage disposal!" Havoc, now in the operating wing, threw everything within reach at Xijax, only to watch it get sucked into his face.

"Cut me a break. I'm trying to reroute the escape pod, and I can't read a damn thing," Lochlan said.

"What, like it's hard?! Hurry the hell up!" Havoc said, pinched between the creature, a desk, and the wall.

"Oh yeah, that's real helpful—Oh shit. Done!" A clap and howl were Lochlan's way of giving himself a high-five. He dashed out of the arsenal, but not before swiping a baton. He barreled down the hall past Vince.

Just as he did, Maynard's scanner went green. The machine was ready. "We're good to go!"

"Coming through!" Havoc shifted into slime again, diving past Xijax like a wave inside a puppet, racing toward the device.

When they were close enough, Vince held out his arm to cast a holding spell, but his magic was weak. Xijax quickly broke the spell. "I am so sick of this place! Hold still!"

Lochlan reeled his cybernetic arm back, energy condensed in a glowing plate beside him. Shield activated and baton in hand, he bounded over the crew for Xijax. "No hard feelings!" He cracked the baton across Xijax's face.

Granted a moment to catch their breath, Havoc fell back. "It's for your own good!" they shouted from behind Lochlan. "For real this time!"

Vince frantically kept attempting a holding spell as Maynard adjusted the machine to aim at his target. Xijax moved too quickly. They had only one shot and risked missing, or worse, hitting Lochlan.

Maynard pulled up the video from the station's security camera and cast a hologram in front of him. The shouting scientists on the recording caught Xijax's attention. Enraged, he made a sharp clicking noise and then lunged toward Maynard. Lochlan and Havoc reached out to protect their captain, abandoning all warnings not to touch Xijax.

"No, don't!" All at once, Vince drained the last of his energy to cast a gust of wind strong enough to blow everyone back. The push stalled Xijax's movement, giving Maynard the perfect window to fire the shot directly into its face. Vince collapsed onto his hands and knees. Every muscle trembled and sweat drenched his thermal wear. He struggled to keep from passing out.

Through blurry vision, he saw Xijax keel over, swaying like he had swallowed something bad. While the rest of the crew gawked at the beginnings of the wormhole falling apart, Lochlan had no interest.

He picked up Havoc into one arm, ran forward, threw Maynard over his shoulder, and scooped Vince under the other arm. He dashed to the escape pod with the crew in arms.

Vince knocked against the wall as the pod launched with an intensity far exceeding the gentle acceleration of a normal shuttle. A cloud of exhaust followed the crew as they careened into space, with the explosion on their tail.

May Flowers

Chapter 23

//Vince

Vince didn't *totally* hate being squeezed between the attractive older men. In fact—if he wasn't so worried about suffocating—this would be like a dream come true.

Lochlan pounded on the door of the cramped escape pod. "Not my baby! You sick son of a bitch!"

Vince squeezed his arm between everyone to poke his husband. "Uh. Loch, I'm right here."

"He's talking about the shuttle." Maynard's shoulders were pushed up to his ears.

From the escape pod's tiny window, Lochlan watched helplessly as the explosion caught the shuttle in its outer edges. The force cracked the hull of the Prometheus into pieces and scattered it across the asteroid field like fiery streamers. "Kill me instead, coward!" Lochlan screamed at where Vince assumed 'up' was.

"Please excuse him," Vince whispered in the same direction.

"Ow! Get off my foot, you gargantuan baby!" Havoc stomped on Lochlan's boot.

"I didn't even know it was our last ride...." With no room to move, Lochlan pivoted in place to face Havoc. "This is *your* fault." They made Maynard and Vince involuntary human shields, shouting and packed in with the fighting sardines.

Within minutes, the crew was back at Leviathan's Luck. The Keel opened to the hangar and the escape pod shot inside, scraping the ground beneath it. A digitized voice reported a safe amount of external oxygen, and the door popped open. Havoc skittered from the escape pod like a roach with the kitchen light switched on and Lochlan chased after them.

Maynard offered Vince a boost and climbed out behind him. "Should we do something about that?" Vince asked.

"No." Once they were back on the ground, Maynard unlatched the release for both their helmets. Vince cringed as he realized Maynard hadn't gone anywhere near the latch when they were at the station. "This is the best way to tire Havoc out before a nap." Maynard clasped his forehead and made a sharp hiss.

"Are you okay?"

"Just a headache." Maynard rubbed his eye. He searched his bag and, with a grumble, scowled toward the ceiling.

"I got it." Vince held his palm to Maynard's pounding forehead. The last wisp of his magic was just enough to soothe the tension.

Maynard closed his eyes, a moan of relief escaped him. "So...about the suit...."

Vince laughed. "I actually really like it. Like, look at me in this thing." He pulled his hand back and struck a pose. "I just needed something to yell about. *But* if it's okay with you, I'd like to make some home improvements."

At the very least, Maynard had to admit Vince had a knack for putting others at ease. "I'll allow it."

"Great! I was going to do it anyway," Vince teased. An amused hum was Maynard's reply and Vince realized he could probably get away with anything if the pain relief kept coming. *Good to know.* "Hey, Maynard?"

"Yes?"

"Thank you. I haven't practiced magic in a while and it was nice to do something good. I mean, this was fucking terrifying but...kind of fun? I definitely get why Lochlan loves it so much."

"I genuinely don't know what we would have done without you." Maynard patted Vince on the shoulder. "I, uhm, I hope you don't mind me saying this, but Lochlan is a very integral part of the team, and, while I would never stand in the way of what makes him happy–"

"He's not going anywhere."

"Good. And about today, I'm feeling a similar sentiment." Maynard's warm smile made way for the lockers.

Vince moved to join Havoc across the Keel, where they were still being chased.

"Okay! Okay, I surrender." They flung their helmet off, held their stomach, and hunched over. "I'm gonna be sick. What if I get in a life ring and collect the hull?"

"Deal." Lochlan removed his helmet. He shook the sweat off his brow and a strong hand brushed through his damp hair. It knocked all the air out of Vince's lungs. Lochlan offered a handshake to Havoc, which was replaced by a pat on the back as they remained stooped over. Under the weight, Havoc collapsed onto the cold ground. Lochlan strolled away to fill their captain in. Maynard probably wouldn't be thrilled about the plan to abuse the ship's safety system but it was probably cheaper than buying a new shuttle and to support Vince's decorating project the crew would need to save any money where they could.

Vince sauntered over to Havoc and settled down beside them. "What are you down here for? You hardly did anything."

Vince kicked Havoc's boot. "Shut up. Magic is exhausting." He unzipped his suit to let the air conditioning in. "So how'd I do?"

"Hmmm." Havoc tucked their arms beneath their head and kicked their leg into the air, crossing it over their knee. "I have notes."

"Well, *I* have got notes too," Vince said, meeting Havoc's inquisitive eyebrow arch with a smirk. "Liiike, when he gets in action mode, Maynard is kinda...." Vince bit his lip.

Havoc gasped. "Couldn't. Agree. More. It's not like I'm here for the conversation. But keep your hands to yourself." They raised a finger at him. "Don't think I haven't noticed that Lochlan is 'kinda' something too. So you're very welcome, by the way, for not sealing the deal on that in all these years."

"Oh, *whatever*." Vince shoved Havoc.

"It would have been easy too with what a cheap whore he is." The teasing trill exploded into sharp laughter between them.

//Lochlan

By the lockers, Maynard and Lochlan talked shuttle. "So, we'll just rebuild. It's not like we haven't had to before." Maynard shoved his helmet inside the metal tub by their lockers and turned on the disinfector. "Damn it, they discontinued those bolts."

Lochlan sat down to remove his boots. "We bought extra, though. I'll take a look around."

"I'll make a mold if I need to." Maynard freed his torso from the top half of his suit. He rolled and rubbed his stiff neck. "So...Vincent is...."

Lochlan grinned. He peeled off the sticky black base layer of thermal clothing. "Like walking porn?"

Maynard choked. "I was going to say *helpful*." He balled his shirt up and threw it into the laundry hamper. "But handsome, too. Objectively speaking." He coughed.

"For a human?" Lochlan tossed his shirt over Maynard's face.

"Man, just leave me alone." Maynard whipped Lochlan with the shirt, sharing in his breezy laughter.

"Now you're not the only one with a partner who's way too pretty for him."

Maynard's lips tightened, although he couldn't disagree. "We are lucky men." They finished undressing, down to just boxers and left it there as they were going to hit the showers anyway.

Lochlan closed his locker and noticed the captain's pursed lips. "Spit it out, Pierce."

"I wanted to see how you felt about a permanent addition to the crew?"

"Oh, so we're taking applications? I want a robot. With lasers." While cleaning his glasses with his shirt, Maynard shot Lochlan a sideways glance. Lochlan laughed. Things had worked out for the best today, regardless of the drama and a husbandly pride puffed up his chest. "It was nice having him around. He did good."

"Magic could come in handy around here and...you two work well together."

"Oh, wait a minute." Lochlan folded his arms. "I know Maynard Percival is not about to tell me he was wrong about something."

Maynard pushed up his glasses. "I'm only wrong if you don't break up."

"You're on, baby." Lochlan poked Maynard in the chest.

Lochlan and Maynard heard their partners laughing and turned towards the new alliance. It finally hit Lochlan how much hell this combo was about to unleash on his life.

"Oh crap!" Lochlan forced everyone's attention. "What day is it?" The realization that the crew had already missed one important date hit him, and he hoped it wasn't too late for the other.

Maynard checked his comm. "May 1st."

"Damn it!" Vince sat up with a pout. "We missed my birthday!"

"*Your* birthday?" Havoc also sat up. "We missed *my* birthday. You're an April baby?"

Vince stood and held out his hand to help Havoc up. "22nd. Taurus."

Havoc took his hand. "13th. Aries."

"Happy Birthday, Your Highness." Vince bent forward.

Havoc returned the bow. "Happy Birthday, Father."

"Happy Birthday to both of you," Lochlan cut in. "Now, if you'll excuse us." He swept Vince off his feet. "I gotta give my husband a few more reasons not to leave me." As Lochlan carried him toward the elevator, he yelled, "Let's go, angel face, we have a bet to win!" All the way, Vince laughed and kicked but Lochlan could still hear Havoc and Maynard from the elevator.

"I'm expecting a birthday present as well, starlight."

"As you wish, darling."

Lochlan remembered a good morning kiss sometime before he'd fallen back asleep. Today, a gentle shake and a frosty nose hadn't woken him. Artificial sunlight draped over his eyes and the heavenly aroma of something from the kitchen pulled him out of bed, surprised to find the spot beside him empty. He got up, craned into a few shallow cracks of his joints, and followed the scent.

He found Vince, standing at the stove, flipping pancakes in a pan. "Well, I think the pool is the best spot. We should cater." He pointed at Maynard with a spatula.

"Agreed." Havoc slapped the counter. "And live music, with a light show, and a fog machine. Oh! And someone that paints faces!"

"Okay...." Maynard scratched the details into a notepad and plugged away at his calculator. "W-well, boys, taking into consideration the fireworks, the champagne tower, and, you know, the shuttle repairs. This is going to be...pretty costly. Could we maybe play our own music?"

Two duo stared blankly at Maynard. "You forgot to write down the bouncy castle," said Havoc, repeatedly tapping the notepad with their nail. Vince nodded.

"This is a party for adults, right?" Maynard asked.

"Oh, and big banner that says 'Happy Birthday Vince and Havoc!'" Vince fanned his hands.

"Havoc and Vince," Havoc edited. Vince scoffed. Thank God they hadn't noticed Lochlan yet. They looked at Maynard, forcing him to play the tie-breaker.

Maynard struggled for a moment, two pairs of eyes burning into him. He weighed the long-term consequences before saying, "W-well, if we were going in alphabetical order...."

Rolling his eyes, Vince saw Lochlan in the hall admiring the view. "Oh Loch, I was just about to get you." He took his husband's hand and led him to sit at the island with the others. Ladling coffee into a mug, Vince carried on with the party conversation. "Fine, *Havoc and Vince*, but I get to pick the color scheme and invite my exes so they can see how amazing my new house is."

"Yes!" Havoc slammed their hands on the counter. "Let's make the clowns suffer." Their brows flew up. "Oh! Clowns?"

"No!" Vince and Maynard shouted.

Vince brought the coffee to Lochlan, who accepted it with a kiss. "Do I get a say in any of this?" Lochlan asked.

"*Ay, mi cielo.*" Vince pinched his husband's cheek. "Of course not."

Above the rim of his cup, an uncontrollable smile stretched across Lochlan's face as he watched his favorite people make their ridiculous plans together. Havoc and Vince really knew how to pile it on, and Maynard seemed on the verge of throwing them out the airlock.

Despite the ludicrous ideas being thrown around and Lochlan's bank account draining before his eyes, this was nice. *Weird*. But nice.

Sᴇᴇ Yᴏᴜ...

//LOG 02...Mercury - Casino Colony

Leviathan's Luck, a motley crew of retirees and spacers, land a gig in their favorite part of the galaxy: Mercury's glitzy Casino Colony. Best weekend ever. They'll expose the Fortuna Hotel for fixing games while taking full advantage of their free accommodations at a luxury hotel.

But with crewmates and longtime couple, Maynard and Havoc, facing a different gamble, the crew is not so sure they've got the winning hand. On his debut mission, Vince hopes to prove his worth by stoking the couple's fire, while Lochlan does all he can to protect his husband from his explosive friends.

Will the crew uncover the secrets of the Fortuna? Can Maynard and Havoc reignite their spark before the odds run out? Are Vince and Lochlan even able to keep their hands off each other? Rouses, roulette, and romantic ruts! The Fortuna hopes you enjoy your stay.

Fast-forward ...

Chapter 10

Maynard reveals Havoc is a prince. The station's security footage shows Dr. F'vr, the lead researcher, trapping the creature inside the operating room with the other researchers. Dr. F'vr then heads for the cockpit before the asteroid hits the station.

Chapter 14

Vince shows that his connection to life energy also allows him to heal.

Acknowledgements

"Life ends at thirty." I don't know how many times I have been told that. Don't get me wrong, if you can manage to do anything before the age of thirty you have every right to celebrate. But personally, my only metric for success is enjoying myself. Maybe it's easy for me to say that as I've been teased for being "born sixty years old" and I have only ever looked forward to getting older. With age comes freedom. Learning to drive, bars with friends, renting a car for road trips, running for office. Well, that last one actually sounds stressful, I'll pass, but I'm certainly looking forward to demolishing a breakfast plate at a senior discount. The IGHOP (Intergalactic House of Pancakes) is gonna hate to see me coming.

No matter how old you are, this series is for anyone who thinks they might be "over the hill." You have survived the climb, the downhill momentum is coming.

Thank you to my fellow writers in the Discord sever for proving to me that adult friendships exist. Thank you to the powers that be for making me a fucking weirdo. Thank you to my friends and family who are forced to sigh and say "yeah" whenever someone points it out.

Now, the big one. Thank you to my spouse who has filled my life with so much light and laughter I couldn't contain it in one book. Who has pulled me out of every spiral, enabled so many bad habits, and who I'd jump into space for.

Let's grow old together.